Justice in an Age

of

Metal and Men

Anthony W. Eichenlaub

ISBN 978-1-950542-00-0

anthonyeichenlaub.com

Cover Art by: Deranged Doctor Design

To my wife,
Carol

Chapter 1

I wore cowboy boots and a dark brown duster made of real oilskin, chewed snuff derived from a real fine tobacco extract, and had Texas Army–issued black metal replacing my whole left arm. The modified Smith and Wesson Model 500 that I hauled around had been manufactured before neural implants were even a thing. I believed in traditional Texas values, right down to my soul. Nobody was above the law, and the law ought to stay out of people's business when it's not needed. As sheriff, my job was to keep it that way.

My name is Jasper Davis Crow. People called me J.D. I was the law around the town of Dead Oak, or at least as close to justice as its people were like to get. It wasn't always enough. Sometimes these tough lands produced some tougher outlaws.

To the average guy on the fringe, a civilization in retreat looks a whole lot like a civilization advancing. That's how it was in independent Texas, anyway. Folks walled themselves up in their big shiny cities while out in the untamed wilderness we struggled to make life out of dirt and justice out of guns. It wasn't the Wild West. *Feral* was probably a better word. It was once tame, but Texan independence, technology, and neglect had ushered it back to the near lawlessness that had heralded its beginnings.

When I met the kid, he wasn't broken. That came later. But he wasn't just some happy boy either. He was strange. He had his own way. Like some tough oak sapling that would one day cast a dark shadow, he was twisted and stunted by the harsh world, but he never did fall. If there's one good thing you could say about him, that kid loved his mama.

Of course, whoever comes later might hear my story and judge what we did. Maybe somebody will learn something from our mistakes or get some form of entertainment from the retelling over the years. I can't say I care for much of any of that. I'll tell the story how I like. I don't believe anyone is going to learn from my mistakes. There are probably too many to sort out. I don't need anybody judging me either. I do that plenty myself.

The call came in early, so the recording was waiting for me when I got into the station. One message, a holo that flickered like a candle ready to burn out showed a frantic-looking farmer's wife yammering about her dead hubby. Seemed he got himself drunk and killed in the middle of the night. It was Daniel Brown. I didn't remember the wife's name at the time, but I knew I could look that up on the way.

That passed for excitement in the town of Dead Oak, Texas. Anyway, it was enough to get me out of bed on a Saturday. With all the shiny tech they sit on over in Austin, you'd think you wouldn't have the need for shithole little towns like this.

There we were anyway.

Dead Oak was a hub for ranchers a couple hundred kilometers around, from what used to be the northern tip of the Chihuahuan desert nearly all the way over to Austin. Since the fall of the American empire a hundred years previous, both the desert and Texas had grown considerably, but the dynamic of rural life had mostly stayed the same. Everything the poor bastards of West Texas scraped out of the dry dirt was shipped through Dead Oak and then straight to that big, shiny city of Austin. Dead Oak was a small town, but it was the place to be for meat, dairy, electricity, or drugs. It wasn't all legal, but you might be surprised at where the federal government of The Republic of Texas drew the line. They sure as hell tried their best to leave Dead Oak alone, which left it to me to take care of the little stuff.

Dead ranchers were little stuff.

I jammed the autopilot button with my three enormous iron fingers, and my police cruiser climbed to fifty meters. Below were the towering black windmills that were such a common sight these days. For a minute, I focused on the horizon that stretched out before me. Then I looked at my reflection in the glass. My hair was still a little more pepper than salt, and lines were forming on my face. They weren't laugh lines. They weren't scowl lines. They were just your average getting-old lines. It happens fast around here. This job was wearing on me.

Looking into the glass, I gave my best scowl to make sure it still worked. This might come in handy. One of my best tools of the trade was that scowl. The other was my friendly attitude and positive outlook, which I was sure to bring out at least once a year. When the general population is armed to the teeth and bulletproof, quite a bit requires nothing more than charm, intimidation, or a clever mixture of the two.

The cruiser dipped to the left. Flying vehicles drove themselves, and I was mostly used to it. Still, my heart skipped when they dropped a few feet or changed direction. Most people didn't pay attention to that sort of thing, but I had seen one too many failed gravity drives and broken logic engines to really trust anything that did the steering for me.

I pulled out my glow cube. It was an old-style gesture holo that I had been using for a decade. Denise. That was her name. Denise Brown. She had five kids and a husband named Daniel on that ranch. The operation was dairy and beef mostly. Part of the Act of Self-Sufficiency after the war drove a lot more dairy down into these parts. Something about sucking milk from Mother Canada's teat didn't sit well with the proud Texan populace.

The ranch was good financially, far as I could tell. They had paid their taxes the previous year and only carried 50 percent of the ranch's value in debt. There was something about some trouble with one of the kids. It looked like minor stuff involving a local gang. I jabbed the power button on my glow cube and stuffed it into my coat pocket.

I picked my hat up off the seat next to me and beat the red dust off of it. I put on the dark brown Stetson and a pair of small, mirrored sunglasses my father gave me when he quit being a lawman so long ago. They were fancy tech stuff, but I almost always left them powered off. I didn't like distractions.

My cruiser had dropped to two meters from the ground, so I hopped out. My boots sent up clouds of hot dust. The blowback from the cruiser pulled at my coat, so I walked a few feet toward the house before pulling my glow cube back out.

The main house was big—Wright-style construction, but probably only about a hundred years old. A quarter mile away I saw a matte black barn the size of a football field. Both buildings had walls that angled in slightly and had rounded corners, like a stubby pyramid. It gave the buildings a stout appearance, but it helped them survive the brutal winds that sometimes raged across those ruined lands.

There was a kid watching me—small, seven or eight, with hair so light it seemed to glow in the sunlight. He stood stiller than I ever thought a kid his age could.

"Howdy," I said. It never hurt to be friendly to kids.

The kid nodded acknowledgement, but just barely. He might not even have known I was there. There were flecks shining in his green eyes. The kid had been enhanced by the wonders of technology. I always hated to see kids changed so young. Structural augments were illegal until you stopped growing. Too many kids were showing up in hospitals outgrowing bones they couldn't afford to upgrade. No way was the federal government of the proud country of Texas going to pay for all that medical nonsense to get that fixed. They just made it illegal. Seemed like big government to me, but it got the job done. Skin and eye enhancements were widely accepted, though. There was usually no surgery involved, so it was generally considered abusive to not enhance kids as young as possible.

"You Francis?" I guessed, based on the info popping up on my cube.

"Frank," the kid whispered.

I crouched down so I could see eye to eye with the kid. He reminded me of something—someone from a long time ago. I looked right into his eyes, but he wasn't looking at mine. He was somehow looking through me.

"Frank, you the man of the house around here?"

He shook his head.

"Well, Frank, you wanna tell me what's happened?"

He shook his head again, almost imperceptibly.

"Son, you ever need any help, you let me know, all right? My name's J.D. It's my job to make sure kids like yourself don't get hurt." I was still looking at his face, but he refused to look back. I felt a lump forming in my throat, but I forced it back. No kid that young should have to experience the death of a loved one.

He didn't nod but he looked me in the eyes for just a second. I saw a flash of purple play across the pupils.

"Well, Frank, is yer ma around?" I stood.

He nodded.

"Where?"

The kid pointed at the barn, so I tipped my hat to him and started walking. My mouth was dry and I desperately needed a drink, preferably a strong one.

The walk was farther than I'd expected. Dry, knee-high grass and uneven ground slowed me down till I stumbled on a packed dirt road running between the house and the barn. It weaved for no discernible reason and made my walk take a good ten minutes. I wasn't in no hurry.

"Mrs. Brown, you in there?" I banged on the wall of the barn a few times. The black wasn't paint. Just like the windmills, the whole thing was covered with a photoelectric paneling. If the wind died, the sun would keep things powered up. If the wind died and it was night, well, they've probably got batteries. If the batteries died, nobody was going to be happy. Most folks made their own power out there. It was as much a commodity as beef or corn, but part of it was subsistence too. People whose bodies were mostly hardware liked to make their own power if they could. It gave them some independence.

"Hold on, hold on," It was a raspy voice. It'd clearly been dried out by years in the heat. It was female but not feminine.

I cracked open a plastic capsule and stuck its contents behind my bottom lip. The tingle of nicotine briefly warmed my jaw. One of the benefits of nanomachines purging poisons and their aftereffects from your system is the way you never build up a resistance to recreational intoxicants. The warm tingle buzzed in my head and brushed my fingertips. I leaned up against the wall next to the eight-meter doorway.

After a while, I heard someone coming. I straightened up and spit out my snuff.

"'Bout time." The woman before me was heavier than would be fashionable in the city, but she wasn't fat. She wasn't tall either. Her age was a mystery, but if I had to guess, I would put her in her early forties. She jutted her square jaw out at me in some sort of defiance that I would have laughed at if I weren't such an outstanding professional. Her straight, brown hair whipped around in the wind as soon as she stepped out of the barn. Her skin was tan in the way that made me think she might just be covered in dust. Could've been augmented skin, but it was too hard to tell through the dirt. She wore the ever-fashionable overalls and real brown leather boots. From her back protruded four long prehensile arms, each ending in a different sort of tool. The back of her neck and her lower back was a full graft of lobstered chrome.

In her left God-given arm, she cradled a baby. One side of her overalls was unbuttoned to give the thing access to a breast. A quick glance at my glow cube tells me that this baby is named Toby. I can't think of any reason to care.

"Ma'am," I tip my hat. "Condolences."

"Condolences, my ass," she spat. "Lazy son of a bitch weren't good for nothin' anyway." The frantic emotion of her video message seemed to have turned into stubborn pragmatism with a touch of anger. It seemed like she had already figured out how to move on, which was good. The ranch wasn't going to wait around for her to mourn.

I nodded. No use arguing.

"He was out there drunk again. Got trampled by the herd, by the look of it."

I nodded again. "Where's the body?"

"He's back behind the barn, 'bout twenty meters south." The baby sucked away at her like there might not be any tomorrow. "Ben's back there. You talk ta him if you need anything." With that, she turned and walked back into the gaping darkness of the barn.

I followed her.

"Just a few questions before I go," I said. "You sure it was an accident?"

"Yup."

Darkness swallowed us and the air became heavy with the humid musk of caged animals. I pulled off my sunglasses and squinted at the shapes moving in the darkness. Big shapes. Longhorns, by the look of them. The modern longhorn stood half again as tall as me and weighed somewhere near two ton. I never could remember if the geneticists had added American bison DNA into the longhorns or if it was the other way around. That was all ancient history. What they got was a giant version of the original Texas longhorn. With bigger being undeniably better than smaller, these animals took over the ranching industry. The modern longhorn was docile, huge, and quite versatile.

"You do dairy?" I saw milking machines hooked to dozens of the beasts.

She stopped and narrowed her eyes at me in response.

"Ma'am?"

"Yeah, we do dairy." She turned and started walking again. "We do diary, beef, leather and out by the house we got some chickens. Just like any other ranch these parts."

I walked in silence. Sometimes people just took a little while to tell their story. She stopped at a small table near the end of one row of penned up cattle. On the table was a pitcher and half of a dozen filthy-looking glasses. She poured two glasses of milk and handed one to me. I nodded a thanks to her and took it. It was sweet and warm—just perfect for such a dry morning.

"Dumb bastard didn't have a problem with the chickens," she said after draining her glass. "They're the only thing that never made us any money."

My eyes had adjusted to the dim light of the barn. I could see the hulking longhorns shifting, agitated by something. I figured it was probably me. I never got along much with animals.

"Drunk son of a bitch was just in the wrong place at the wrong time. Shoulda known just before sunrise is when the cattle comes back to the barn. Happens every damn day." She spat on the dirt floor. "Goes on, though, doesn't it?"

I nodded.

"Well, you best get out there and finish what you need to do so we can burn and bury the son of a bitch."

The longhorns were settling down again. The rhythmic noise of milking machines was the only noise for some time. I walked to the back door of the barn slowly, breathing in the humid stink of a hundred giant cattle. They were the foundation of Texas. Operations like this all over the country were all that kept those cities from chaos and anarchy. There probably wasn't a single city dweller who knew it, though. Funny how that worked.

Before I left the barn I turned and glanced at Denise one last time. She had finished feeding her baby. Throughout the barn there were dozens of popping noises as milking machines disconnected. I smiled at the idea of people resembling their pets. I guess that works for some of these ranchers too.

The grass out in back of the barn was tall but not dry yet. I plucked a long strand and stuck it between my teeth. I smiled, sure that it would be an easy morning. Folks die all the time. Accidents or old age don't give me much trouble. I just check a box and scan the area and let the family take care of the cleanup. Take it or leave it—that's about as much involvement as people wanted their government to have.

I walked twenty meters from the barn and looked around. Must have been the spot, but I didn't see anything. Fat, irritating flies drifted in the sharp morning light, so I knew I was close.

The kid was nowhere in sight.

The ground back there was packed reddish clay. It was hard like concrete shaped to look like trampled mud. With the toe of my boot, I poked at the hoof print of a longhorn.

"We grow 'em pretty big." The voice sounded like that of a boy who desperately wished his voice was deeper.

I turned and saw him sitting on the hard ground. He had the gangly limbs and almost-muscles of an eleven-year-old with sandy blond hair spiked into seven long spears. He had a wrap-around mirrored lens covering his eyes and a poncho that shifted colors like a chameleon when he moved.

"I bet." I turned back to my work. I didn't think I was going to need the kid's help and I got the impression that he didn't like me much.

Then I saw it behind a thick stand of grass. All I needed to do was follow the flies. The body had been crushed all right. I waved my natural hand through the controls on my glow cube, cursing when it didn't work. One of the problems with my partially enhanced self was that tech didn't always work. Some days were better than others. I switched hands and clumsily operated the cube with my three huge, industrial clamp-like metal fingers. I scanned the body and got a full work-up of the surrounding area. Never hurts to run full procedure, even in the case of an obvious accident. Like I said, I'm a sucker for tradition.

The area was covered with giant hoof prints. Some looked fresh, but I could tell by a slight wear around the edges of the print that the mud had molded them days ago. Also, it hadn't rained in two weeks. The scan confirmed that the guy was saturated with alcohol, and decomposition put the time of death just before sunrise. Cattle coming in just before morning must have trampled the pathetic passed-out rancher.

"It wasn't an accident." The kid was talking again. I ignored him.

Daniel was crushed bad enough that the face was ruined. I leaned in close to get a good look, but there wasn't much to see. He was just a smashed pulp at this point. I took out a metal vial and scooped up a blood sample. The vial plugged into the top of my glow cube, which then went through a series of tests.

There was a hoof print on what was left of his face and severe crushing to the arms and torso. There was a bend in his right leg that was nothing like natural. Most likely, he'd been killed and then trampled for a good long time.

"It wasn't. Someone killed my pa. I'm telling you."

There was plenty of blood too. The hole in the guy's shoulder looked a lot like something an upset longhorn might make. The abdomen was torn. Blood and feces mixed, but I didn't smell it in the dry heat. I couldn't smell anything.

The flies did, though. They had already started to swarm on this fresh feast. They caked the corpse's eyes and gut. They swarmed around the kid and me, checking to see if we might be good for eating soon too. We might be, I thought, but not yet. There was a crow circling overhead that might have had the same idea. I figured it might be a good idea to finish up before the coyotes and buzzards showed up to the party.

My glow cube dinged a positive ID on the body. It was Daniel, all right. Daniel Brown of Dead Oak, Texas. Registered as married and joint owner of the Brown Ranch.

"Sorry, kid. It's yer pa."

"You listening to me? I fucking know it's my pa. Someone killed him. You gonna do anything?"

I let the glow cube finish a scan of the area. Then I turned it off. I had seen everything I needed for the day. It was a long flight back, and I didn't feel like dawdling in that dry heat all day.

The kid stood up and walked over to me.

I raised an eyebrow at him and picked my teeth with a blade of grass. The kid stepped up, right in my face. Brave, considering I probably outweighed him by a good twenty kilos.

"C'mon sheriff. You slacking or what? Look at the goddamn body." His hair spikes almost came up to my chin.

"Saw it. Looks like your pa got himself killed."

Nothing in the evidence supported the theory that Daniel Brown was murdered. It was, however, perfectly natural for boys of a certain age to cling to such ideas as a way to cope with the tragedy and disappointment. Coping was fine, I believed, but the sort of coping that I suspected the kid was gearing up for most likely involved guns and revenge. Any sort of questioning might further support his wild theory, and while I would have appreciated his perspective on the matter, I just didn't want to risk it.

In short, I had somehow managed to survive until that day without figuring out that being dismissive and aloof was not a wise or effective way to handle boys of a certain age.

"Shit, they just hire stupid ones to be the law these days, huh?"

I looked at him, stared at him right in the eyes. The kid was mad. I brought two fingers up to my lips and gave out my loudest whistle. "Kid," I said. "I looked at the body. Your drunk pa got himself trampled by your damn cattle."

The kid looked at me hard, like he wanted to hit me. I was ready for it. I would have dropped him to the ground. I don't hold back for kids. Some of the augments these punks have are as dangerous as they are freaky.

But he backed down. "It was murder, jackass."

My cruiser was coming fast, responding to my whistle. I raised my army-issue black metal arm and stared at the kid. Right on cue, the cruiser dropped a line, and I felt the prehensile grappler as it latched onto my arm and yanked me into the air. It lifted me into the passenger seat. My job was done there.

Being a sheriff was hard work sometimes. It was dangerous and people didn't always like you. Sometimes it was fighting hard for justice day after day in the unduly hot deserts of southern Texas. Some days it was just gritting your teeth and muscling through as fate and hatred and technology all work against you as best they can.

Some days it was easy.

A sea of black windmills in the rearview mirror swallowed the Brown Ranch. Despite my best efforts, a smile crept across my face. It was an open and shut case. No violence, no detective work, no gangsters or punks. I figured that this was an easy case and it was going to be an easy day.

I was wrong.

Damn wrong.

Chapter 2

"It's murder."

I glared up at Contrisha Chin, the new deputy, and spat a wad of snuff into a can on my desk.

After visiting the Brown Ranch, I had made a few rounds through town and settled down in my dark office. The walls were gray cinderblock, with all the decorations you'd expect from a small-town sheriff's office. There was an overfull trashcan next to a sleek metal desk. The place smelled of stale tobacco smoke and electricity, and for good reason. The office was part of a small underground complex built to withstand any of form of natural disaster and all but the worst man-made ones.

I was mad as hell. Trish was in the doorway of my office, trying to ruin what might have been the start of a very good nap.

The girl was easy on the eyes; she had all the right proportions that a city girl was likely to have. Her skin was a deep mocha. Her hair was nearly black and curly in a way that even the fancy tech of the city wasn't likely to have simulated. Of course, the plastic sheen of her skin told me it was not completely unaltered, but chances were she was sporting her original tone, and I appreciated that.

Her arms and fingers were wholly artificial, an artistic idea of what perfect limbs ought to look like. I hated Trish. She was just a kid who'd been sent up from Austin the week before. I got this feeling about Trish whenever she talked. It was like breaking glass and screaming puppies. It gave me a headache. She annoyed me, but more importantly I knew it was odd for Austin to send reinforcements or even acknowledge our existence.

I rubbed the bridge of my nose and pulled in a deep breath. It was smoky in the dingy office. Trish was smoking one of those skinny little cigarettes that people smoke when they want to look like they're smoking but don't give a damn about the contents of their drug of choice. It was a sweet smoke—smelled like cinnamon. It also gave me a headache.

My eyes wandered to the top drawer of my desk. The need for a drink was almost overpowering, but I wasn't going to get anything out with Trish in the room.

My glow cube sat in a shiny, black cradle on the desk. I knew Trish was accessing it wirelessly through her brain implant, but I had to look at things the old-fashioned way. A detailed hologram of the murder scene was projected above the desk. I fumbled with the controls and managed to zoom the image in to get a closer look at the victim's ruined face.

There were burn marks, dozens of them all over the guy's skin and clothes. I'd missed it before because they weren't deep. I couldn't tell what they were from, but they shouldn't have been there. The guy had been trampled, not burned. I leaned forward and the image flickered.

"The burn marks are one thing, but check out the heart," Trish said. She got a far-off look and I saw the deep green irises of her eyes flash bright for a second in the dim room.

Her voice didn't actually sound like broken glass. It was a fine voice—light and untroubled by the cruel heat. It just happened to be a significantly higher pitch than I would have liked to hear at that particular moment. I had no problems with female companionship, though I did prefer the company of men. Contrisha Chin just had a voice that bothered me. I ground my teeth together and tried my best to ignore the voice but acknowledge the words.

I waved my hologram so that it would display the crushed and mangled innards of Daniel Brown. It didn't. I tried again.

"You have the feed set too low." Trish smirked.

A person may have interpreted her comment as nothing but helpful, but in my mood I heard mockery. I swiped an exaggerated form of the gesture again, hoping it might work. Nothing happened.

"These older units were notoriously touchy."

I scowled at her and she winced. Using my bulky metal hand I jammed three fingers into the image and yanked it into position, zooming in closer by splaying all three finger apart. The grisly image of a crushed human heart hovered between us.

"Looks pretty mangled to me."

"Yeah, but look *how* it's mangled. Oxygen levels are low in the muscle tissue, like he had a heart attack. Also, the puncture on the left ventricle is from that broken rib. Judging from the damage, though, this happened after the heart had already stopped beating."

I grunted and peered at the image as if I could see exactly what she was talking about. "So, it's a heart attack?"

"Yeah, yeah! Exactly!" Somehow she failed to see how this meant it still wasn't murder. "A heart attack when this guy had a full neurocranial augment and emo-regulating nanomachines? Doesn't that seem fishy to you?"

I leaned back in my dingy leather chair and put my feet up on the desk. "Nope."

"Seriously?" She gave me a look that only reaffirmed my feelings for her.

"Seriously." I put my hat on over my face to block out the light and folded my hands over my chest.

"Look, J.D., at the burns, along with the heart problems, and did you notice his mem chip is missing? Those don't just vanish, you know. I think this guy was tortured with fire and possibly roughed up a little. When that didn't work, they hacked his augments and jacked him from the inside, causing the heart attack."

I gave it a long pause. "Sure."

She was right, of course.

That pissed me off.

"Also," she continued, "he wasn't drunk. There was plenty of alcohol in his stomach, but it hadn't penetrated to the rest of his body or his brain. It looked like his nannies were purging the blood stream and keeping him from getting drunk. So, the alcohol was there, but drunkenness was not the reason that he got trampled by his herd of longhorns."

Another long pause. "Sure."

"Well, you gonna do anything? Open an investigation?"

"Sure." I decided several minutes previously that I was going to open an investigation. I was just being difficult to piss her off. There was no reason I had to be the only one pissed off.

Her jaw was set hard. Her lips were so tight I could bounce bullets off of them. That might have been true. I wondered how that might work. Modified skin could come in all sorts of different forms, but it was almost always bulletproof. It'd probably still break her sparkling teeth. A weak smile crossed my face. I was normally a decent guy, but something about pretty upstarts from the city with mysterious agendas found the worst in me.

"What's the first step, boss?" she asked, emphasizing *boss* in a way that might've contained an ounce or two of sarcasm.

"Not a lot to go on. Might want to start with figuring out who didn't like the guy. You check the Hub, where he did his business, and I'll ask down at the Goat."

Her eyes narrowed. She knew I was giving her the harder of the two assignments. The Hub was where every rancher from a few hundred kilometers around came to turn his goods into cash. It was the only place in town that was busy twenty-four hours a day. The place was crawling with all sorts of traders, merchants, and anybody who had something to sell. Most of it was legal, but every once in a while I had to go bust something up. It had been a while since there'd been any trouble down there. Over the years, I had earned a sort of respect among the locals, but they knew not to say too much when I was around. I was sending Trish in because chances were that people there would be more likely to talk to her. Something about being pretty and young had a certain effect on most of these ranchers.

I sat for a bit and let the silence inform her that it was time to leave. She did, but she wasn't happy.

There was a certain kind of logic swimming around my head. The Dry Goat was a tavern. If I went there right away I'd be tempted to get a drink and I didn't think it would be a good idea, considering the job I was going to need to do.

This logic, bad as it was, prompted me to open the top drawer of my desk and pulled out an unmarked steel flask. I bit my lip. I wanted it in the way a person wants to fall right after he's walked off a cliff.

I stood and walked to the office door and closed it. Hanging on a hook behind the door was my duster, so I reached in the pocket and pulled out a small metal marble. It was an e-cuff, one of the few pieces of tech that I was genuinely good at operating. In truth, those e-cuffs were my only real physical advantage over the teched-out goons of feral Texas. I gave it a twist and attached it to the metal of my arm. It snapped on as if it were a really strong magnet, which might've actually been what it was as far as I knew.

A jolt ran through my body. Every muscle contracted, even those that had to fight other muscles to do it. After a second I regained a little movement, but my left arm—the black metal one—dropped to my side, completely limp. E-cuffs were great for disabling augmented criminals. They were also pretty good at disabling the nannies that prevent an honest augmented human from properly feeling the effects of alcohol. Replacing an arm is easy, but getting it to integrate nicely into a living being is not such an easy task. My one replaced arm involved a modified clavicle, spinal implants, and a dozen other minor structural changes designed to keep the heavy lifting that I can do from tearing the rest of me apart. It also involved about a million tiny machines that cleaned my blood, reversed minor tissue damage, and kept my neural pathways as clear as they could possibly be from the poisons and the toxicity that all of that integrated tech brought on. Those were the nannies, or nanomachines. There was a nanny factory somewhere in my hardware half that kept my blood swimming with the things.

I unscrewed the flask with one hand and took a swig, fighting the reflexive sneer that good, strong liquor usually summons. I didn't quite succeed, but I followed it with a deep second gulp anyway.

By the third swig I was starting to feel better.

Trish would probably take hours at the Hub, so I knocked back another burning mouthful. What was her story anyway? The best answer I could come up with was that she probably screwed something up terribly in Austin, and she was out here serving some sort of penance. I knew I needed to be back to the station by the time she returned so there would be no awkward questions. She didn't need to know how this job affected me. I thought about how meeting that kid on the ranch had brought back so many bad memories.

Bad thoughts led to more bad thoughts. I wasn't a happy drunk. I closed my eyes, but images of the war flashed before me. I opened my eyes, but I saw myself staring at

Daniel Brown's mangled heart. The holo flickered at me and ignored my futile attempts to shut it down with my one working hand.

So, I stared at it and took a deep drink. I closed my eyes again, but the grisly image of Mr. Brown's heart was seared onto the backs of my eyelids. I thought another drink might erase it, but it didn't. I thought one more drink might move me to action—get me up and after Brown's killer. It didn't. One drink after another failed, but I was nothing if not stubborn.

Then the flask was empty and I nearly fell out of my chair in surprise.

An hour had passed. I swore and tried to shake my fist at the clock, but it was my left fist and it didn't move. I cursed at the damn metal thing for a full minute before figuring out what was going on.

I pushed my thumbprint against the E-cuff. It beeped, turned green, and fell off.

My heart raced in my chest, and I heard its incessant drumming drowning out the world. My panicked lungs wouldn't stop trying to pull in more air, even though they were full. I couldn't exhale. White-hot fire shot through my chest. My muscles seized up and my skin began to tingle.

Dry heaves wracked me as I lay in the fetal position on the concrete floor.

The nannies tended to kick into full gear when they powered back up to find a person full of poison.

"Jesus," I swore at nobody in particular—myself, maybe. The room had stopped spinning and the unpleasant feeling of dizziness was being slowly replaced with a gut-wrenching self-hatred. I swallowed it. As far as I could tell, that was the best thing to do with it.

I stood up, grabbed my duster, and picked up my hat from the floor, where I hadn't remembered dropping it. I needed to make a quick trip down to the Dry Goat and make it back before Trish did.

Like any addict, I never really understood why I drank. It didn't make sense to me why I sometimes needed the drink to do my job. Maybe it was because it was a hard job that was full of futility and frustration. Really, I think I believed that deep down there must have been some sense of pride or duty in my soul. There must've been some love of country that drove my need for justice. After all, I had sacrificed so much for that ideal. There must have been something that I somehow thought would come back to me if I drank. It was bad logic. I felt nothing when I drank.

All I felt was numb.

Chapter 3

The station was quiet. Outside of my office and to the left was the jail. A short hallway and heavy steel door led to a longer hallway featuring several holding cells featuring various levels of ridiculously heavy security. Some of the modders that I sometimes had to contain there were so jacked up that we couldn't expect to hold them in a standard box of metal and concrete. The jail was empty that day. One of my goals as the sheriff was to keep it that way. Any criminal worthy of real punishment was either executed or shipped to the city for a trial. Dead Oak was too small to have its own judge, or that was what the officials in the city told us. Those who weren't sent away to trial were usually fined and released quickly.

To the right was a powdered glass doorway, which I passed through before realizing my mistake. Deputy Johnson was there, losing some sort of argument.

"I'm sorry, Miss Meriwether," he said. "There just isn't anything we can do. Pastor Sharpe hasn't broken any laws, far as I can tell."

There were others in the waiting area. A man I recognized as Old Jack was spinning a coin on an end table, while his grandson Young Jack and a deeply tanned stranger watched. Old Jack and Young Jack were here far too often, usually with complaints about Jack, who most people called Just Jack. You wouldn't want to call him that to his face. Just Jack made a living out of distilling liquor and raising rabbits. Liquor tended to give Just Jack an ugly temper, and he never did agree with the way Old Jack took over custody of Young Jack. Also, he hated rabbits.

"Well, son," said Bea Meriwether, an elderly woman in a blue flowered dress. She was a thin-lipped woman who appeared to be made entirely of sharp edges and loose flesh. "You'd best think of something you can do. That man won't leave us alone at the center."

"Have you talked to the owner?" Johnson asked.

"Ain't gonna do you no good, Bea," said Old Jack.

"Yes, I have," Miss Meriwether said. "Don't you think I wouldn't go there first?" She stepped up and leaned on the counter. "He won't do a thing either. You folks're all a bunch of impotent bastards, you know that?" Her pitch was getting dangerously high.

The stranger pulled out a long pipe and began tapping it to release the remains of its contents. The man was wrinkled and his hair was white, but his eyes sparkled with an amusement I normally associated with youth.

I stepped forward to rescue Johnson. My head was clearer now. The nannies had almost erased the effects of my binge.

"Ma'am—"

"Don't you *ma'am* me, sonny! I want that Baptist locked up!"

"Um," I said. "We might not have a legal action against him, but I will go talk to the man—see if maybe we can work something out." It was a waste of time, but sometimes a sheriff could step in and mitigate situations like this.

"Talk to him? You going to just talk to him then it's better? I hope that talk comes with some hot lead and some knuckles."

"Well, there's no need—"

"Or maybe just baptize the son of a bitch. Clean away some of that sin of his."

"Ma'am—"

"Don't you *ma'am* me! You even listenin'? Now, you get out there and take care a this problem or I'm coming right back here tomorrow." With that, she huffed out the door, leaving Johnson and I staring.

Old Jack spun a second coin and Young Jack, who couldn't have been more than three years old, clapped and giggled. The stranger lit his pipe and the room filled with a deep, musky smoke.

"Thanks, boss," said Johnson.

"My pleasure." I tipped my hat at Johnson, not envying him his position at the front desk. Ned Johnson was a deputy I could respect. He was clean-cut and old enough to remember a day when Texas Rangers were mostly human. This was the sort of square-jawed, chiseled guy most women and some of us men hoped to someday end up with. He did his job well, and he had respect for the people he'd sworn to protect. That might have been why they always walked all over him.

With a nod to Old Jack and a polite smile at the stranger, I made my leave of the station. Sunlight drove its way into my skull as I stepped through the entrance to the underground station. I slipped on my sunglasses and tipped my head down. The taste of the red dust came back almost immediately, making me think again of how thirsty I was. I always found it strange how all of that drinking didn't help my thirst one bit.

The streets were busier than normal. People were trying to get their business finished before the day got really hot. There was a storm coming too. The air had a sort of heaviness that only preceded big thunderstorms. I idly wondered when it was expected to hit. Cars of all shapes and sizes were cruising down the main road through town, some hovering a half meter above the ground and others taking a higher altitude. In the skies, autopilot sorted things out, but down here in the town people used good old-fashioned right-of-way rules. There were no vehicles touching the packed dirt road. Cheap antigrav all but ended that practice long before I was ever born.

Two boys from across town were huddled in the entrance to a general store across from the station. I recognized them but didn't remember their names, so I settled for tipping my hat in their direction. One of them nodded solemnly back, but the other turned and pretended not to see me. When I ran into their mother a few blocks later, I tipped her off to their location. Boys need their freedom, but a mother needs to know where her kids are when a storm's coming.

Most buildings in town were fashioned after the Navajo hogan, a domelike building that was used for generations before European architecture took over. As the Chihuahuan Desert spread north and east, desert dwellers from what was once Arizona and New Mexico moved south to occupy it. As the megastorms of the new climate swept away inferior European buildings, the old, more practical styles moved back in. The modern hogan was the perfect desert residence. They were built from solid stone, and they ranged in size from the traditional two-meters tall to greater than twenty. Usually the modern version also included an underground component, which satisfied the need for a cool, dry place to hang your hat and take off your boots.

The town of Dead Oak was a cluster of a few hundred of these hogans gathered around an enormous oak. As the name implies, the oak had been dead for generations, preserved by a sentimental townspeople and the calcification of a dangerously harsh environment. It wasn't hard to understand why people loved that tree. It stood strong against the brutal storms and desiccating winds, growing stronger for all the hard times nature and man sent at it. People saw it as a metaphor for their own lives. It seemed fitting, then, that the tree had been dead for years.

The Dry Goat was one of the few remaining structures in town that was fully above ground. The Goat was a one-story flat-topped rectangle. It was gray concrete block and a polished granite facade facing what passed for a street. The entrance was a genuine honest-to-goodness double swinging door, like you'd expect from some ancient American Western movie. Inside was something else.

The main room was lit by a strangely pulsing tube of glowing light that wove its way around the ceiling, down pillars, and along the walls. Its hypnotic movement was dizzying and more than a little distracting, especially given the fact that every surface of the place seemed to be some sort of polished or mirrored steel. Smoke hung heavy and stale in the morning glow of the place. The thrum of the latest music craze filled the air. It was the sort of music a person felt rather than heard, and it did not improve my headache.

I paused for a moment at the door. Those watching might have been convinced that this was a dramatic choice designed to give the criminal element a chance to shake in its collective boots. It wasn't. I needed a moment to let my eyes adjust. Nobody there would even remember what that was like. Their eyes all sparkled with the telltale flash of heavy augmentation.

Once I was reasonably sure I wouldn't run into anything on the way, I made my way up to the bar. Like everything else here, it was steel and plastic, with stools to match. I bellied up and took a look at the rows of identical unlabeled bottles. I never knew what was in them, but the bartender seemed to know his business. I motioned with a finger to get his attention.

"'Sup, sheriff?" He was a short fellow who wore a metal-rimmed monocle that I suspected helped him identify bottles. He was heavily modified, with black—really black—skin and an intricate circuit-board pattern tattooed in glowing blue. His fingernails were shining steel, as were his teeth. Two mirrored steel horns protruded from his hairless head.

"'Morning, Mr. Lucifer." I had a polite relationship with the man, though I trusted him about as much as I believed his real name was Lucifer. "Hoping you could help me out."

"You needing a drink on this fine morning?"

"Nope." Not anymore. "Just looking for info on a man who frequents your fine establishment." With my eyes fully adjusted, I scanned the main room to see who else was around. There were a couple of clean-cut men wearing gray suits and sunglasses right in the middle of the room. Out of place, but I pegged them as out-of-towners.

Behind them I saw a trio of modders. They were nothing but kids, really; the oldest was probably twenty. I had seen these guys around, even busted them a few times for minor trouble. They were all spikes and steel, but most of it was for show.

Three stools down from me was a woman in a blue dress. Her long, dark hair was pulled back into a trio of braids. At her feet was a duffel bag and a walking stick with some feathers attached to the top. She was drinking something clear on ice. When I saw her I politely smiled and removed my hat. Sometimes it pays to be polite in the company of women. This woman just frowned and turned away. I decided that she was about the last person I wanted to question in this establishment.

Lucifer leaned in close. "You talking about Clayton Dewitt? Because, my friend, as much as I respect you I am not going to tell you what that fine gentleman is dealing to my esteemed patrons." His wide grin showed me a dozen shining teeth.

"No." I leaned in close. "I'm talking about Daniel Brown. Comes in here sometimes."

His grin widened.

My jaw tightened and a scowl crossed my face. "Spit it out."

"Well." The bartender glanced at the three modders in the corner. "The man was not without his enemies."

Lucifer gave me a devilish grin and pulled a bottle off of the shelf. With a flourish, he poured me a drink in a tiny shot glass. He'd told me enough and I could tell when the man wasn't going to let anything else slip. The sharp scent of bourbon reached my nose and I felt a touch of the nausea.

My feet hit the floor and I pulled myself away from the drink. That damn devil would have loved to hold this weakness over me, but I wouldn't give him the chance.

I gave the modders a good look as I placed my hat back on my head. They were looking back at me now, watching me a little too closely. Their expressions were tense. I had a split second to make a decision and I decided to take the soft approach. I relaxed my jaw and slipped out the old pleasant smile. There was nothing threatening about me. I took a step forward.

They ran.

They split up. Two went for the back and one for the front.

I went after the guy who was headed for the front. He was closer and I nearly caught him as he shouldered the door open.

Intense sunlight blinded me as I followed him outside. I heard the kid's footsteps to the left, so I bolted in that direction.

My vision adjusted and I saw him only a few meters ahead of me.

He was fast. His legs were heavily modded, possibly full replacements. At the corner, he leapt into the air, avoiding the traffic by jumping over the main line of low flying vehicles.

I leaned into it. My lungs worked hard. Legs burned. My duster flapped behind me. I sped up, hoping to stay close enough to at least figure out where the kid was heading.

I ducked under a hovering car and stumbled forward, blasted by its blowback. I kept to my feet, but the traffic had slowed me down. I was pumping hard now, sprinting with everything I had and almost keeping up to the freakish kid. He was ten meters ahead, but I felt like I was gaining.

A screeching noise echoed through the town from somewhere behind me. It was metal on metal. The kid turned back to look, and I made up half the distance between us.

My heart pounded in my chest, threatening to burst. My lungs tore at the heavy air.

The kid looked at the sky behind me, then his focus fell to me again.

The bastard wasn't even breathing hard.

He smiled. His chromed teeth shone in the morning sun.

He stopped.

I lunged forward, sure that he couldn't get away now.

He jumped straight up. My fingers closed on air.

I skidded onto the ground. Above, one of the other modders hovered on a jet bike. The bike was a tiny one-man skidder. It wavered and loped around a little. It was not designed for that much weight. They were only about four meters up.

"I..." I gasped for air. "I'm not trying to arrest you!"

The kids laughed. The one steering the bike shouted down, "And we're not trying to get arrested!"

My breath was returning, but I stayed down on the ground. "It's about Daniel Brown. The rancher."

"Seems if it was important you'd have run faster," smiled the kid who had easily outrun me.

All pretense of the friendly sheriff dropped from my face. "Say that again, kid."

"I said." The kid laughed. "If you want an answer, maybe you should run a little faster."

I clenched my fist and ground my teeth. I didn't much like kids who thought their tech made them better than regular people. I didn't like kids who disrespected authority. I really didn't like kids who disrespected me. "I didn't hear you," I said through my teeth.

They laughed but there was something they didn't know.

"I said," the kid started, enunciating each word with a flourish.

I slid my boot underneath myself and jumped as hard as I could. They'd drifted down far enough that I was just able to reach the pegs with my right hand.

As soon as I gripped the foot peg, I realized my mistake. I couldn't get my e-cuffs out very well with my metal arm, and I couldn't hold on as well with my human one.

Also, my human fingers were a bit more vulnerable to getting stepped on.

The bike, which had been loping, now started to downright fail. Its engine strained against the extra weight and it started to drop.

The runner squirmed and stomped at my fingers. It was all I could do to keep from getting them crushed.

The other kid cranked on the bars and leaned hard. The bike drifted sideways, scraping me against the slanted side of the nearest dome. A blast of smoke and fire burst from an auxiliary thruster and the bike pulsed upward. The heat scorched the sleeve of my duster, but it didn't penetrate to the skin.

I scraped desperately at the wall, trying to get some purchase, but the wall was smooth stone all the way up. The kid with the modded legs stopped stomping at me and focused on holding onto his friend. Somehow the tiny bike still had enough lift to keep rising with all three of us.

Giving up on holding us all down, I swung my left arm up, hoping to find another handhold.

I did. My hand clamped hard onto a pipe jutting from the side of the bike. We had reached the top of the dome, and the bike seemed to still be rising. The tips of my boots were all that touched the stone structure, and we were still sliding sideways.

"One last chance, boys!" I yelled.

The kid on the back started stomping at me again, like he had forgotten I was there.

It was too late. I'd already let go with my right hand.

I thrust my hand in my pocket and grabbed half a dozen e-cuffs.

The bike swung up over the busy street.

The e-cuffs hummed in my clenched fist. I pulled them back for a throw.

The runner's eyes got wide. "*Hijo de puta,*" he swore.

Just then, my handhold broke.

The solid steel of passing traffic cushioned my fall. I bounced off of one car, then rolled and landed face down on the dirt road. The e-cuffs rolled uselessly from my hand as I gasped desperately.

Dazed, I forced myself up on my hands and knees. My head swum and everything seemed a little fuzzy. A vague awareness of traffic zooming past muddled into my consciousness.

I looked up just in time to raise my arm to defect a sedan that was coming in far too low.

The last things I remembered before I blacked out were intense pain and the crippling humiliation of defeat. I'd like to say that the pain was the worse of the two, but I wouldn't want to lie.

Chapter 4

There are jackals everywhere. They snarl and stink of piss and rot. The things circle me. They eye me, probably trying to decide if I'll fight or if I'm just another snack.

With great effort, I force myself to my feet—unsteady at first, crouched low so I can stay upright.

My arm is missing—the metal one. It's gone completely and in its place the sleeve is folded and pinned neatly. I'm in the desert.

The jackals inch closer.

I yell to frighten them, but they act as if I don't exist. Their eyes are locked on something else—something behind me.

They're looking at Francis.

The boy from the farm sits perfectly still at my feet. He stares into the distance, eyes flashing in the hot afternoon sun.

I throw a rock at the bravest jackal, but others circle. I spin to meet them, but I can't frighten them all. One nips at Francis, tearing his shirt and leaving a scratch on his arm.

But it's not Francis anymore. It's Conrad. My brother looks up at me with tears in his eyes.

I stare, stunned.

The jackals pour in from all sides. One tears into Conrad's leg. Another rips at his neck. Conrad stares forward, reacting to nothing.

I grab at them with my good hand. I pull one mangy creature after another, but I lack the strength to kill them. Those that I toss aside just come forward again. The space they leave is instantly filled.

Then there's nothing but bones. Strips of flesh still trail from them as the jackals rip them free and run back into the desert.

I see my father, then. He looks at me with sad eyes and shakes his grizzled head. He turns his back on me and leaves. I don't bother to plead with him to come back.

Cruel consciousness hit me harder than some fiber-fabricated sedan ever could. A piercing ache arced through the back of my skull and pulsed through the length of my spine.

Worse, though, was a new feeling right in the center of my chest. It was a tightness that I couldn't recall ever having felt before. It made it hard to breath, so I gasped hot gulps of heavy air. It didn't help. There was something else too. Big drops of water ran from my eyes, blinding me. Blinking back the tears seemed to just encourage more. I felt weak.

Fumbling a little, I managed to put on my sunglasses.

Someone had dragged me out of the street and leaned me up against a hogan that sported a wooden sign with the words "Cornsley Dentistry" displayed in fabulously flourished letters. Half a dozen meters from where I ached, the sedan was parked at an odd angle. Its front sported an impressively caved-in fender and hood. This was to be expected when fabbed fiber went up against black metal. I'd have felt bad for it if the black metal in this scenario hadn't been attached to me. Above, the street traffic continued as normal, whizzing by as if nothing had happened.

The dirt road featured one twenty-meter, sheriff-sized skid mark. My coat corroborated that evidence. The skid had worn all the way through it in a couple places. I winced as I poked at the resulting road rash. There wasn't any serious damage that I could see, but it stung just as much as you might suspect it would.

A stocky man emerged from the building holding a glass of water. It was Frederick Cornsley, the dentist. He had a mustache that made him look like a well-muscled walrus in a white lab coat. "Good morning, Sheriff Crow," he said as he held the water out for me.

I took a sip. "Mornin'."

"Saw you fall, sir. You all right?" He was shifting his weight nervously.

A stick-thin woman in an ankle-length green dress walked by, eyeing me like she was afraid she might step in me if she wasn't careful.

"Yeah, I'm fine." I gritted my teeth and forced myself to my feet. Every part of my natural body hurt. It was a dull ache—not the sharp pain of serious damage. "I'm no *sir*, though." I drained the glass and handed it back to him. The water tasted faintly of chlorine and cherries.

"No, of course, sir, um Mr. Crow." He was flustered.

"You see what happened?"

"Yes, sir."

I let it slide. "You know those boys who flew away?"

"Well, I'd seen them around before."

"Know where I can find them?"

A kid a couple meters from me shouted across the street to a friend, who crossed to join him. They were a couple of impish little guys, and I made sure to keep an eye on them so they wouldn't get too close. Their tanned skin looked enhanced and they wore black feathers in their hair. They were creeping closer to the wrecked sedan, seemingly unaware of my presence.

"No." Frederick was backing away slowly.

I could probably have asked him pointed questions for hours. I didn't. Instead, I scowled at the man and silently counted to ten.

"No, sir. I mean, yes, sir. I mean, Mr. Crow." I had only made it to four. "It's just, I've seen them around the old junction."

"You expect they'll be there now?"

"Maybe later tonight. I don't usually see them during the day. It's usually around dusk that I see them. There's a couple dozen or so. Sometimes I hear them talk. Their leader sounds like she's some kind of goddess."

I grunt in the affirmative. "Her name?"

"I...I don't know."

There was a hint of fear in his eyes, but his story was convincing enough. I believed that he didn't know anything else, but I suspected he was involved in something illegal. There was no good reason for a dentist to be at the old junction. It had been shut down for a decade.

"It's just I don't want them to think I talked."

I raised an eyebrow.

"I have enough problems with graffiti here, you know, without their help."

"The information's much appreciated, Dr. Cornsley. I'll do my best to not let on who it came from."

He retreated into his building. By then the authorities had arrived. I recognized the officers and waved one of them over. The other one began the work of extracting the driver from a foam safety bubble.

"Officer Anders," I said.

"Good morning, sheriff."

"Make sure there's no trouble for that driver. Wasn't his fault."

He raised an eyebrow.

"I was chasing down some kids and ran into some trouble. Fell into the street and this guy just happened to be in the wrong place at the wrong time."

"You all right?"

"'Bout as good as can be expected."

"Better, by the look of it."

I raised my left arm and turned it around a few times. The polish was scratched, but the arm was otherwise unharmed. "Well, officer, the good government of Texas does tend to put some high-quality equipment into her soldiers."

With a nod, he returned to his work.

The Dry Goat was a dead end. With all the commotion, any leads that might have been sticking around would have fled—not that there were any to start with. Those kids would need to be chased down, of course, but from the sound of it I wasn't going to find them until it got dark out. If they were smart, they might have even skipped town. I was willing to bet they weren't that smart.

The station was only a few blocks away. I cursed myself for not whistling for a ride or maybe some backup during that chase. What made me think I could chase down a kid half my age with augmented legs and a flying motorbike? Pride, I guessed. I was looking forward to spending the afternoon resting in my office. I licked my dry lips, but my stomach turned at the thought of another drink.

About a block from the station, a thundering black patrol car pulled up beside me and ruined my plans. It was Trish. Sunlight shone off of the polished curves of that beautiful black convertible, making the whole thing look ablaze. We don't get vehicles like that out here. Trish had brought it with her when she was transferred from Austin. The outside was all glitter and show, but even I had to admit the thing had some muscle. I could feel the rumbling of the engine in my chest as it idled next to me. Heaven only knew what kind of bureaucratic nightmare Trish would've had to walk through to get it transferred with her.

She smirked from the passenger seat in a way that did nothing to improve my opinion of her.

I kept walking.

She drifted the car forward to keep pace with me. "Rough day?"

"Not yet."

The car was low and the top was down, so I grabbed the side and pulled myself into the seat next to Trish. It felt good to be off my feet. The ache had faded some, but I was tired and getting hungry. Red dust spread across anything I touched inside her otherwise spotless cruiser.

As soon as I was settled, the cruiser lifted gently into the sky.

I looked down at the entrance to the station. A man was leaning against the wall next to the door, wearing a black three-piece suit and a black Stetson. He was smoking something like a small cigar. The wind whisked the smoke from his face as fast as he made it.

"Friend of yours?" I asked.

Trish glanced down but didn't answer. She closed her eyes for a second, and soon the car was speeding up and out of town. She had used a neural signal to give the car coordinates. It was a parlor trick—nothing fancy. As far as I could tell, it wasn't any easier than speaking the instructions or pushing a button.

The convertible was comfortable, designed to seat four people facing each other. The seating was plush and blue, more comfortable than the chair in my office. There were no visible manual controls, but a panel between two of the seats looked like it might slide back if the right command were given. I wondered how this car would ever hold a hostile criminal. My guess was that prisoner transport was not a consideration when this cruiser was designed.

I interlaced my fingers behind my head, leaned back, and put my feet up on the plush seat in front of me. Deputy Trish's glare threatened to bore a hole in the side of my head.

The cruiser rose to about sixty meters. I briefly wondered where we were headed, but I decided that Trish would say something once she was ready. My refusal to initiate the conversation seemed to bother her, which at the time seemed like an added bonus. I was uncomfortable, knowing she had probably figured out something I hadn't. After all, I knew if justice were going to be done, it would be done by me. Information gave her control and that made me nervous.

Still, there was more than one way to show her who was in charge. I waited.

"The city," she finally said. "We're going to Austin. I have a lead."

I raised an eyebrow, feeling a little jealous that her investigation had done so much better than mine.

"It's a little complicated." She spoke slowly, like I was slow or something. "Plus, it involves some tech. So, listen to the whole thing, all right?"

I nodded.

"Do you know anything about the dairy industry?"

"Nope."

"Neither does anyone else. Nobody cares." She reached under her seat and slid out a shiny steel bin, straddling it. She opened it to reveal dozens of odds and ends. Most of it was tech that I didn't recognize. At first it seemed like this was part of the story, but soon I realized she was only reorganizing it.

She continued. "Modern dairy production works much the same as it has since the invention of teats. A cow gives birth, triggering milk production. Then she's milked for a certain amount of time until she's ready to start the cycle all over again. The side effect of this process is that we get a nice beef industry and the cattle production can easily meet the needs of a growing herd."

I scanned the horizon and tried to emit my very best "I don't give a damn" vibe.

"This is all great for a growing industry, but things are changing. Most people don't eat beef anymore. Cattle live longer and are productive longer. So, calf production isn't always beneficial. It's a waste of resources, and resources aren't all that great around here." She punctuated her point with a wicked-looking ceramic blade.

"True." I stared at her, absolutely bewildered by her decision to reorganize her belongings rather than sit back and enjoy the view.

"Well, then something new came along in the form of a specialized E-chip. You've heard of those, right?" The black blade whistled as she gestured, but she put it down when I gave her an annoyed look.

"Yup. Ran into a couple of junkies pushing emo a couple months ago."

"Right, so junkies use it to tap into other people's emotions. The transmitter gets some specialized hardware and some coordinated nannies. It all works over the sub-quantum net, so range is incredible. The junkies ingest the nannies and start feeling whatever emotions the transmitter feels. More advanced systems are more selective, allowing better control. The nannies replicate the effects of hormones and brain signals. It can sometimes be dangerous, but by itself it isn't illegal."

Below, the plains gave way to the distinct meander of the Colorado Husk, formerly referred to as the Colorado River. We cut across the sharp turns of the once wide river, which was now choked with dust and brambles. Windmills were fewer out there. Power lines crossed the landscape, but almost nobody lived in the ruined waste close to the city.

"Unless they start jacking into people who don't give consent," I said, pulling myself away from the tragedy below.

"People do that?"

"Don't ask me why." I sat up. She had me interested. Not only was she a city girl who knew about the dairy industry, but she also seemed to know more than I did. "In my opinion, there are too many damn emotions as it is. What I never understood was why they need the transmitter at all. Why can't they just set the damn things to 'happy' and leave them there?"

"Most of us have brains that are too complex for anything that simple." She was getting into it. As she grew more excited, the pitch of her voice grew more irritating. "It might work once, but then you adjust. Can you ever remember two times you were happy and it was the exact same feeling? It never is, it turns out. So, when you start feeling the same emotion pushed down on you, you recognize it on some instinctive level, and in recognizing it you reject it."

I stared off at the landscape, squinting into the morning sun. I was less interested in the technology and more interested in trying to remember two times when I had been truly happy.

Trish shook her head. "The Browns had recently started a program to use similar tech on cattle. The emotive response can be used to trigger milk production. It's a little strange, but ends up being better and cheaper than dosing the cattle with drugs to accomplish the same goals."

Denise Brown had an E-chip. She had been nursing her baby right there in the barn. I wondered what any of this had to do with the murder. I raised my eyebrow and motioned for Trish to continue.

"The process is controversial. Many producers feel that this will destroy an industry that has existed for thousands of years. It generates milk, which is profitable, but it doesn't produce more cattle. So, beef production drops and it might be harder to maintain the dairy herd." She was making a stack of shining, gold disks on the floor next to the bin at her feet. They were either holograph projectors or ammo for some bizarre weapon. I couldn't tell which.

"That's just stupid. Nobody's going to murder anyone for that."

She took a deep breath like the kind a person takes when they need to calm themselves after a great annoyance. "However," she said through her teeth. "There are only three big dairy distributers: Quintech, Gateway Industries, and Goodwin. Quintech and Gateway already refused to sell his product. The last one, Goodwin Dairy, dropped the Brown farm about a month ago."

"Then murdered him?"

"Probably not."

I looked at her questioningly.

"His finances didn't take a hit at all."

"Finances?"

"Yes. He kept right on making money, even though no officially recognized distributer would touch his goods."

"Then someone else was distributing it," I speculated. "And that person likes to murder people."

Trish grabbed the stack of disks and slammed them back into the bin. They scattered as they fell and ended up worse off than before. Her jaw tightened and her eyes got hard.

"It's a lead, Crow," she said. "We talk to Goodwin Dairy and find out why they dropped him, then we track down whoever is really distributing his goods. Shady deals like this can lead to people dying in mysterious circumstances."

"My pa always likes to say its people who murder people—not money or drugs or love. Just people."

"Well, your pa must be one fine lawman to be so clever."

After a pause, I said, "No, ma'am, he isn't. He's a decent bounty hunter, though."

"I see." The reputation for bounty hunters was not good. The laws that governed them were even more lax than most laws in Texas. "People need a motive, though. We figure out the motive and we find the killer."

"Murdered over milk."

Her eyes hardened even more, though I hadn't thought it possible. "Yes, J.D. Murdered over milk. It's a lead. Did you get any leads at your bar or did you just get a good buzz?"

I pulled a toothpick from the pocket of my duster and stuck it in my mouth. The kids had almost been a lead, only there really was no reason to believe that they were in any way connected. "I did get a lead, as a matter of fact," I lied.

It was her turn to look expectantly.

Twenty minutes of awkward silence passed before I saw the gleam of Austin on the horizon. From a distance it was beautiful—a fleck of silver surrounded by the pulsing dull blackness of the windmill fields.

"The kids," I finally said. "The ones I was chasing. They could have been involved."

At first she didn't answer, and I thought maybe she was not listening. Then she said, "Really." It was somewhere between a statement and a question.

"Round dusk I think I can catch them near the old junction. It's a long shot."

"I'm going to go out on a limb and guess that you didn't get vid of the whole thing?" Her voice was dry now. Her eyes locked with mine. "We could get some glasses for you, you know—special sunglasses that record what you see?"

"I have some."

She perked up. "Were they on?"

"Nope."

She clenched her fists. She was tolerating me but just barely. I made a mental note to switch the glasses on the next time something happened. A video of the event would have made identification easy, and it probably would have saved us a trip into a dangerous gang confrontation.

I didn't like the idea of being tracked on video. Computers could compile enormous dossiers on each of us, and there was no way to know who got that information. Presumably, it was someone very, very powerful. I felt that it was important to the health of society that someone could avoid such close scrutiny. Freedom from the establishment was one of those principle ideals that the great Republic of Texas was founded on. It's what I'd fought for twenty years ago in the Civil War that nearly broke Texas apart. It was something I still believed in, even though by many standards I represented the establishment. Out there, I was the one people needed to hide from.

I explained none of that to Trish. How could I? She was half machine and half city girl—her brain was probably jacked into some government feed at all times. Even if I decided that I could trust her there was no way to know who else was listening. The Republic of Texas was a democracy, but city votes outnumbered those of ranchers by thousands to one. Those in charge would not want to hear about any desire for freedom from the establishment. Also, she would think I was crazy. After all, when the outlanders fought the city twenty years ago, it had been a draw. Nobody could win, so on paper we all came out even. If only it had worked out a little more like that in reality.

48

Technically speaking, I was her boss. She would do what I asked, whether or not I explained my motives.

Austin drew closer. The hundred-meter windwall rose before us. Polished metal spires stretched like a hundred webbed fingers clawing at the sky. Between them, the mesh crisscrossed like black spider webs. We could hear them as we got closer, the howl of wind reached a deafening pitch.

"Why do we have to come all this way?" I was shouting over the noise of the wind as we passed through a gap in the webbing. "Can't you just make some calls?"

She shook her head. "I tried. You know how it is. The city likes to pretend like you don't even exist out there. They just barely recognize that there is any law out there. If we're going to get any information, we're going to have to apply a little charm." She gave her best smile. It was, I admit, quite lovely. "Which works best in person."

I smiled. "So, that's why you brought me?"

She looked at me with those dry, humorless eyes. "Exactly."

We passed through the last layer of windwall and Austin spread out before us. The noise of the wall dropped away, eclipsed by the roar of the city. Streams of cars floated in layer after layer above and below us. Shining curved buildings stretched high above us into the sky. The sharp tang of electricity and iron assaulted me. There were people everywhere.

My heart raced and my palms began to sweat. It felt like the city's weight was crushing me. There was so much activity. A dozen twisted humans crawled up the side of a nearby building. Cars zoomed close—too close. Above, flashing neon advertised tech and women and food all at once. Each display lasted only a second before rapidly pulsing to something else. With augmented senses, many people could easily handle this overload, but not me.

I flipped on my sunglasses and ordered them to start filtering. The ads disappeared—completely erased from view. Activity and noise faded into nothing more than a dull background blur.

Trish smirked at me, her eyes glowing as we passed through a building's shadow. She was enjoying this. She was back in her element and my discomfort seemed to amuse her.

"Let's get this over with," I said through clenched teeth. "Sooner we're out of here, the better."

It's funny how sometimes we say things that are truer than we know.

When I didn't hear a response from Trish, I tore my gaze from the overly busy landscape and looked over to her. Another wave of panic surged over me; the weight of the city pushed down on me again.

Deputy Chin had disappeared.

Chapter 5

If a person counts "Howdy" as a sentence, then I had managed to deeply offend a man in a metal suit named Chester with only three sentences.

He looked like he was ready to hit me, and he didn't look like the hitting type. He looked more like the snivel-and-grovel type, with a touch of delete-your-data-stream-later. The small, black-haired man sported a wispy mustache and something they call an accountant's jack. It reminded me a lot of the prehensile tool arms that old Ma Brown had, but this ran straight into the man's spine and probably consisted of nothing more than a data line. It was plugged into the wall next to him. Flecks of light flickered in his eyes from time to time. I was certain that he hadn't bothered to stop working just to talk to some lowlife like me.

After Trish had inexplicably vanished her cruiser had landed me near the work entrance to the Goodwin Dairy distribution center, halfway up a building called the Alamo Center. The place was a hive of activity with cargo tubs coming and going in dozens of different directions and some sort of bottling operation happening inside. Trish had used her connections in the city to get me a meeting with the angry little man, which I discovered as soon as I was able to track down someone who resembled a receptionist. The whole business bothered me, and I couldn't help but think it was all just Trish playing a mean trick to make me feel uncomfortable. Also, I was having trouble understanding what good we could get from this.

"Listen, wastelander," Chester said. "Big Milk, as you call it, happens to be some pretty big business. Blood nannies can stay functional for weeks in the stuff—so yes, people still drink it on a regular basis. Without it, we'd all need to have integrated nanny fabbers like they did in the old days. So, you backwards bumpkin, if you have nothing else to do but insult the proud tradition of this company, then you can just show yourself the door."

His eyes glazed over and I was certain his attention had left the room.

What happened next was not entirely my fault. The room seemed like it was designed specifically to make me uncomfortable. The walls were lined with fake plants—like somebody enjoyed the idea of plants but thought the theme would be improved if plants were brushed aluminum and copper. The walls were a mixture of enameled steel and white glowing glass. Above the glass was a network of wires, tubing, and some sort of mechanical arm. The table between the skinny man and me was heavy steel and mahogany. My coat hung in the corner on one of several metal protrusions that may or may not have been put there for that purpose. My hat was still comfortably on my head and my sunglasses were securely in place, recording everything.

The security guards outside had checked me over, but for some reason they had let me keep my revolver. They had smiled at it as if it were some toy gun, which might have been the case, given the armored skin that most city folk seemed to have. Mr. Skinny across the table was no exception. The plastic shine of his face gave the impression of something far better fortified than the average unmodified human. My gun wasn't of any use anyway. It wasn't loaded.

It was then that the rage hit me. It was frustrating getting nowhere with the milk man, but the rage didn't come from that. This rage came from nowhere.

It bubbled in the pit of my stomach. My jaw clenched and my fists gripped my chair so hard that one of the aluminum arms bent. I stared down at my black metal hand and willed it to release, which it did reluctantly.

The man still stared off into space.

I stood, sending my chair flying across the room. I pounded my metal fist onto the table, cracking the mahogany and denting metal.

That got his attention.

He looked with confusion into my rage-filled eyes.

I reached forward with my right hand, grabbed a handful of his greasy black hair, and slammed his head into the desk. Hard.

"Listen, milkman," I said, surprised at the angry growl of my voice. "I need to know why you dropped the Brown account. Now."

I couldn't see the expression on his face. "Okay, okay." I felt him struggle to raise his head, but I held it down. "The Brown account... I don't know. There have been a lot of reports of contamination."

"What was the reason?" My grip tightened.

"I don't know. We have independent agents checking the field—"

"Don't give me that shit," I said. I gave his head another good pound against the table.

"Well..."

I leaned over to look at his face. I didn't like what I saw.

The bastard was smiling.

He had been stalling.

I dropped his head and turned just in time to see two teched-out goons shoulder their way into the room. These guys were more metal than man, and they looked like they had been big to start with. The first one looked at me with glowing red orbs and raised something that could be nothing other than a weapon.

I rolled backward over the desk and dropped into cover. The goon fired the weapon—a pulse of energy hit the desk and sent numbness through my hand where I was still touching it. I could hear a low hum from the other side of the room.

The weasel of an accountant twitched a couple times and then slumped to the ground.

I heard a *clump, clump* as the second goon moved forward.

"Come out with your hands up," one of them intoned.

I shook my hand to get the feeling back into it. "I'm a lawman."

There was a pause. "Then stand up, sir, and we'll talk about it."

The rage was completely gone now, replaced by a touch of confusion. What had I done?

The weasel's arm hung limply next to me, so I grabbed it, put a hat on it, and held it up. Soon as it crossed the top of the desk, a pulse of yellow filled the room.

"Fuck!" I yelled. My arm went numb again, as did the entire right half of my body. Again, I heard a low hum rising steadily in pitch. Whatever they were using to shoot at me had to recharge.

It was my only chance to escape.

I jumped, intending to roll back over the desk at the closest goon. My right leg was still numb, though, and didn't respond properly. I stumbled over, landing in a heap on the other side.

Still, it surprised them. Goon 1 raised his weapon at me, but it was still charging. Goon 2 moved forward, leaning down to either restrain or murder me.

I rolled back and kicked hard at Goon 2's face. I landed a solid blow to the jaw. It stopped him for all of one second.

He lunged, reaching for me with his etched steel arms.

I slid under him and pushed, directing his momentum at his unsuspecting ally. The two crashed together in a heap. I quickly snatched my coat from its hook and made a run for it.

I was halfway to the door when a flash of yellow filled the room.

I turned to look at the two goons, still tangled together on the floor. Goon 1's weapon was pointed at me, trails of yellow particulate streaming from its business end.

It hadn't hit me.

The air between us shimmered and crackled like static on a broken vid.

Then Trish was there with wide and unfocused eyes. She'd appeared from nowhere. She swayed back and forth, and then toppled toward me.

I would like to say that I caught her. It would have been the gentlemanly thing to do. Unfortunately, I wasn't fast enough. I barely got a hand under her to soften her face's impact with the ground.

Instead, I stood and sputtered, "You've been here all along?"

She was in no condition to respond.

I scooped her up, surprised at how light she was, and tossed her over my shoulder. I ran out of the door and down the hall before the two thugs could follow.

Reinforced glass doors opened up into chaos. My heart raced and I bit my lower lip. To the left, I saw bins carrying polished steel containers—dozens of them. Workers were placing them in these bins, then the bins would float themselves by some unknown route to destinations elsewhere in the warehouse. People were running everywhere. To the right, there was a robotic wall. Hundreds of arms jutted from its surface, each performing some mundane task over and over: filling bottles and kegs, welding, sanding, molding. I couldn't even hope to understand everything that was going on.

The center of the room was something that I supposed must be the control center. A twenty-meter array of displays, dials, and buttons dominated the space. Just outside of its technological magnificence there were other, lesser altars of steel glory, each with its own worshipper.

There's a funny thing about chaos. As a lawman, I hate the stuff. My instinct is to control it—make it go away. When I can't, it rankles me. It gets under my skin and burrows holes in my skull. Standing there in that warehouse brought back that headache.

It wasn't chaos, though. It was a well-orchestrated machine. Every piece of this hustle and bustle understood just exactly what it was there for and how to interact with the pieces around it. A hustler wouldn't bustle any more than a bee would fetch slippers. They all had their places, machines and men, and it was getting hard to tell them apart.

Everything had its place but me.

A noise behind me spurred me into action. I ducked to the left and down a fiber mesh staircase. Twenty meters below, the warehouse floor seethed with movement—a vast sea of machine and humanity. I could get lost down there, I thought.

The goons burst through the doors just as I reached the warehouse floor. I ducked low and pushed into the crowd.

But I didn't fit. First from the left and then from the right, people bumped into me. One jarred me so hard I nearly dropped Trish. The far-off gaze of a worker snapped into focus for long enough to give me an offended, questioning look. I pushed past him and moved on. Trish stirred on my shoulder.

The other side of the warehouse was the docks. If I could make it there, we would be able to summon Trish's cruiser, and we'd disappear into the city.

I glanced back over my shoulder. The goons had multiplied, now there were half a dozen of them swarming the upper levels of the warehouse. They pointed down at me, tracking me as I parted the seas below. Not only was I failing to blend in, but I was also pretty much making it impossible for them to miss me.

I needed a new plan. I put Trish down next to a console that jutted up from the grated floor.

"C'mon. Wake up," I muttered at her. She made no response other than fluttering her eyelids.

I was out of breath and just about finished running. So what if they shot me with their stun gun? They would probably let me go once they figured out who I was, right?

One of the job requirement of the Texas lawman is unwavering, undeniable stubbornness. It's something of a point of pride. Sure, logic dictated surrender. Fighting my way out was both stupid and nearly impossible. Yet, there I was.

I stood and scanned the upper levels. One, two, three of them had guns pointed at me. Three more goons were muscling their way through the crowd below. One of them was Goon 2. His face still bore the anger of the recently humiliated.

My jaw jutted forward and my fists went up. I shrugged my coat off onto the floor and faced Goon 2.

"What's your name, son?" I asked as he stepped forward. He was sizing me up.

"Jenkins. Yours?"

"You can call me Sheriff Crow."

The crowd around us parted, but it didn't stop. It just flowed around us, giving us a little space to work with.

Jenkins was about as opposite to me as I expected a person could get. My arm was black metal, an alloy designed and produced by the Texan Armed Forces. His augments were shiny, like etched steel or possibly painted plastic. His right arm and both legs were covered in exoskeleton. Most of his face was too. His skin had the sheen of something new and improved, and much of it had been replaced by something that looked like a cross between fish scales and burned meat. I just had the regular sort of skin. It had done me fine all my life. Apart from a few scars, I think I had taken pretty good care of it.

Trish groaned at my feet. Maybe she was starting to wake up or maybe she was just dreaming of headaches and hot baths. Either way, I didn't think she'd be ready for action. I had to take care of this myself.

"You know," I said to Jenkins, "in the old days, people would walk ten paces and then shoot each other."

He slowly circled left, looking me right in the eyes as if we were going to hypnotize me into submission.

I lowered my voice so that only he would hear me. "Everyone's watching this time, Jenkins. Wouldn't want to get humiliated again, would you?"

The fleshiest parts of his face got just a little redder. He kept circling.

"You know who you're dealing with, don't you?" I asked. "Special Forces Ranger, Natural Division. I took down bots like you during the war. You probably got that data dump already, though, didn't you?"

The stare continued. His head was bobbing back and forth.

"I'm not a natural anymore, though, son. I've been fighting kids like you for twenty years."

Finally, he responded. "I don't want to have to hurt you, old man." He opened and closed his oversized exoskeleton fists. He definitely had reach on me—strength too, probably.

He took a swipe with his left, but I dipped back out of reach.

I smiled at him tauntingly.

He lost all focus and lunged. I grabbed his right arm with my left and yanked it as hard as I could. He stumbled forward, but he was ready this time. He kept his feet underneath him and made an awkward attempt at a backhand. I dodged and we separated again.

In the distance, through the doors of the warehouse, I saw something. It looked like Trish's cruiser. I fought off the urge to look back at Trish, but I figured she must be awake by now. If I could just stall another minute, we might be able to make an escape.

"Of course," I said, "I don't have my brain hooked up to some fancy network. I just need to make some guesses about who you might be."

He raised an eyebrow.

"My guess is you grew up fatter than the other boys, so you got picked on a lot." His jaw tightened. "You eventually found that your size would let you win most fights, so you pretty much just let it do all the work. No need to train for any real skills."

He made a wide roundhouse with open fingers. It was probably supposed to be a grab, but instead of ducking back I stepped forward. My augmented arm formed a box so that he wouldn't be able to just bear hug me to death. My face was inches from his. We locked gazes.

"Jenkins," I said. "Back off and let us leave. Save yourself the humiliation."

I shifted a little and grabbed his shoulder from the armpit. It was armored in heavy metal, but I had a good grip. I started to squeeze.

There was panic in his eyes as he began to feel the pressure. The metalwork covering his shoulder screeched as it bent and twisted. Still, he didn't back down. With his left fist, he jabbed at my ribs but I was too close. He couldn't get any force into it—not even with his strength. The exoskeleton prevented him from properly reaching me.

So he fell on me.

Jenkins made a sudden push forward, launching his whole body at me. He landed on me hard. A sharp stab of pain ran up my leg and his weight pinned my left arm against my chest. It was a sorry way to win the fight, but still I knew I was beat.

"Who's humiliated now?" Jenkins's face was awkwardly smashed up against mine.

I made a futile push to try to get him off of me. My arm was strong, but people are just so damn awkward. Every time I pushed part of him, he would compensate with another. His fellow goons were laughing about it, which did not improve my mood.

"Well," I said. "I suppose you beat me fair. What's your plan now?"

The fleshy parts of his face got a quizzical expression.

"Sometimes in the heat of battle we fail to think ahead," I spoke so that only he could hear me. "For instance, if you so much as move I'm going to be at you again."

Jenkins shifted his weight and another bolt of pain ran through my leg.

"No shame in asking your friends for help, is there?" I had to admit to myself that Jenkins had earned a little of my respect. Still, my own pride demanded that I mock him just a little bit more. "I mean, you already won the contest of mass, so who out there can doubt your ability?"

With his jaw hardened, Jenkins boomed, "Take him down."

Laughter dropped hard into silence. Above, Trish's looming cruiser blackened the light out. Out of the corner of my eye, I saw her fly into the air.

There was a shout from far away—a cry of pain that might have been mine. I saw a yellow light and then nothing.

Chapter 6

I was not accustomed to the inside of a jail cell. It was cold, sterile, and insultingly Spartan. There was an open metal toilet in one corner and a bare mattress in another. One wall featured a doorway, really more of a gap with a shining barrier of light. I had no idea what that light did, but I expected I didn't want to touch them. So I did. My fingernail sent up a wisp of white smoke.

Some time had passed. I later found out it was something like an hour, but there was no indication when I woke up. It felt like days. My head hurt. My duster, sidearm, and hat were missing—not that they'd have done me much good in there. My white shirt was torn from when I'd skidded through my duster that morning. Blood spattered the otherwise pristine cotton. The wound still stung, but the throbbing of my bruised knee nicely overshadowed the pain.

I tried to piece together what had happened because I didn't want to think about what the future might hold. Trish's cruiser had arrived. Had she chosen not to swing down to pick me up or had she somehow still been captured? I decided it was unlikely that she had been killed or captured. There was no solid evidence to support my belief, but that's what I believed anyway. Trish was a mystery, and mysteries tended to require faith.

Still, something didn't fit. Why had Trish gone invisible and dumped me in the middle of trouble in the first place? Was it just a mean bit of city humor? Maybe she had some other motive. Maybe there was a reason she didn't want to be seen. The more I tried to figure her out, the more mysterious she became.

"The Browns need justice," I muttered to nobody in particular. "They need justice and ain't nobody going to bring it but me." I repeated it to myself, again and again, hoping to find some reserve of strength in it. No solution presented itself. My distorted reflection in the metal floor just stared back up at me like it was expecting me to do something. Hard as I tried, I couldn't think of anything to do.

Eventually, a reprieve showed up in the form of the greasy accountant whom I'd recently bludgeoned. His pale face was already showing dark bruising along one side and his movements were awkward and uncomfortable. He looked just about exactly how I felt.

My anger was gone. When I looked at him I felt sorry for what I had done. I felt pity and remorse. Why had I done that to him?

Before I had a chance to really give it some thought, he spoke in a quiet voice. "They should never let you people past the wall, for your own sake."

I stood to meet the man, determined not to show him how helpless I felt. Less than a meter separated us, but those shimmering lights still kept us apart. I took his confidence as another clue that I probably ought not to reach through the field to shake his hand.

"My apologies," I said.

"If only I could accept an apology so easily."

I stood quietly. If he had something to say, then I was just going to let him say it. No need to get too wordy. Jenkins and another man in an exoskeleton lingered in the back of the other room. Out there I could also see computer jacks and terminals, two shiny metal doors, and a big red button behind some glass. My guess was that I didn't want that button to be pushed.

"It seems you had an accomplice." The man shifted uncomfortably tenderly flexing his jaw. "Prettier and smarter than yourself."

I nodded. There was no use denying it.

"The law is quite clear on the matter. You can either be sentenced to a life of labor or a simple, painless death. Accuser's choice."

"Life of labor?" I couldn't keep silent anymore. The gravity of my situation was becoming clearer.

"Or a painless death. Due to recent events, I am leaning toward death."

"For roughing you up a little?"

"No, of course not." The man took a step back. "Tell me, what is your name?"

"Jasper Davis Crow," I said. "Sheriff J.D. Crow, if you happen to like titles."

He apparently did not. "Well, Mr. Crow, it seems your accomplice—"

"Who is also an officer of the law."

"Your accomplice stole some very important information from us. Trade secrets are not to be trifled with in today's economy."

"I bet."

"You will tell me who your accomplice is and who the two of you work for."

"We don't work for anyone," I said. "We're chasing down a smuggling operation from one of your former producers."

"The information is lost. We understand that there is no way to contain it once it leaves our systems. We want that woman, though. We suspect she has stolen from us before and we suspect she will do it again. Give her to us and we might be able to deal."

"Son, you're going to need a better deal than what you're offering if you want me to give you anything."

A tail snaked out from the back of the man's head, accessing some panel on the outside of the doorway that I couldn't see. The field dropped and the man stepped forward. The top of his head came up to my shoulders, but his glare was something fierce.

He poked a finger into my chest. "You are not in a position to negotiate, wastelander, you decrepit waste of food and fuel. You are nothing to us. You should have stayed out of Austin like your waste of a life depended on it."

"You listen to me," I said in a low growl. "I am a sheriff—lawman of Dead Oak and purveyor of the justice you seem to have lost sight of. There's no dealing in justice. The guilty pay and the innocent walk."

He blinked at me.

I was angry again, not at the man before me, but at the whole damn city. Everything was wrong here. Everything had been twisted and broken long ago.

Something was making my left arm weak. I could still move it, but it wasn't strong enough to assault a moth, let alone the weasel in front of me.

My right arm didn't have that problem.

I grabbed a handful of the man's shirt, lifted him, and pushed him forward.

The second goon sprung instantly to action, but Jenkins stood still. He just smiled.

I held the gibbering fool between the goon and me. In the corner of the room I saw my coat, hat, and gun. I made my way over to them and scooped them up with my left arm as best I could.

The goon ducked left, but I was too fast. He seemed too afraid to hurt my living shield.

He shifted right but so did I.

Jenkins moved almost casually to a console and pushed a few buttons.

"Put me down!" Now that he was in mortal danger for the second time in one day, the man's voice had reached an insane pitch. All pity that I harbored for the man was long gone. I shoved him backward, letting him tangle up the goon for a second while I pulled out my gun.

The silver door slit away, revealing a tiny elevator.

Trish stepped out, smiling like this was all extremely funny. It was not.

With casual abandon, Trish shot yellow pulses of energy at the goon and the man. She turned the weapon on Jenkins, but he raised his hands in a plea for peace.

"Really?" Trish said.

"I know what you're doing."

Trish shot him.

"It'll be better for his career this way." She waved me into the elevator. "His boss would never believe him if we'd left him alone."

I nodded, shrugged on my coat, and stood quietly as she sent the elevator upward.

Trish demonstrated her inability to handle silence. "Things work differently where you're from, don't they?"

"Yup."

"I mean, all you needed to do was walk in, talk the guy, then walk out. I would have gotten all the information if you hadn't picked a fight, and then we could've moved on."

I nodded.

"But you had to get physical with the owner's son and knock fists with his bodyguards? What the hell, J.D.?"

"Owner's son?"

"Yes, J.D. That was the owner's son's head that you randomly pounded into unconsciousness. Chester Goodwin. He's kind of a jerk, but I don't know that he deserved to be treated like that. We *are* law enforcement, you know."

"Are we, Trish? I know I am, but what exactly did you say your credentials were?"

"It's not that simple out here." She got a distant look. Just as she was fixing to say something, the elevator dinged and opened onto a roof that stretched out for about twenty meters. Wind tugged at us as we stepped out, but we didn't have to go far to reach Trish's car. Soon we were speeding away from Goodwin Dairy and down into the boiling smog of the turbulent city.

"So, where are we headed now, deputy? Out of the city, I hope."

"One more stop," said Trish. "Tarrytown."

I didn't like how that sounded. I was ready to be done with the city for the day, preferably for the rest of my life. One more stop. I could do just one more.

Chapter 7

Nobody's story exists in a vacuum. Sometimes a tale has to get around to itself in a roundabout fashion. This is the story of a boy forever changed, and that's where this is going. We met many times over the years, but it's those first few that mattered most. To understand what happened to that boy, you need to understand the world he lived in, and you need to understand me.

I was tough but not the toughest. I was fast but not the fastest by a long shot. Any punk with a bit of money to burn at the mod shop was faster, stronger, and smarter than me.

It wasn't just the city folk. It was all of them. My people, the natural people of the world, were a dying breed, and thanks to the Texan Armed Forces, I couldn't even count myself pure. You might have called me human, and most people would have said my heart was in the right place, but things were different back then. Nobody lived without tech—not even those of us who despised it.

"You want a history lesson?" Trish asked as we visited yet another rundown hovel in the place she'd called Tarrytown.

In response, I blew a smoke ring, watching as it left the environmentally controlled bubble to be destroyed by the wind. She didn't get the hint.

"Tarrytown was the only Austin neighborhood to correctly predict the weather changes that would lead to the superstorms. They built the very first windwall a decade before the first storm ripped through the city." She smiled. "Since theirs was the only neighborhood saved from the storm, they were the only neighborhood that didn't get rebuilt during the Rise from Ashes of the late twenty-first century."

"Therefore, it's a shithole."

"Exactly." Trish gave me a serious look. "Dirty, old, abandoned. This is the place the government forgets about. It's where criminals come to live out their days and poke each other with sharp objects."

"Wonderful."

"Don't fuck this up, boss."

I glared.

"They don't need your judgment. People don't believe in justice here."

"I won't judge."

"Yes, you will."

"I'll keep it to myself."

She gave me a doubtful look.

"I'll try."

"I guess that's all I can expect."

"Why do I get the feeling you think you're my boss?"

"Maybe I should be."

I gave her the scowl, a good one. As much as I appreciated her rescuing me from the Goodwin jail, something still bothered me about her. Unfortunately, if I wanted any sort of justice for the dead rancher, I'd have to rely on her some more. We weren't any closer to solving the murder.

"Look," she said. "Around here, I'm the expert. I ran in these circles for years before relocating to your backwater village. I have contacts here and I understand the local customs. Just keep your head low and hope nobody notices you're a fleshy weakling."

"Listen, deputy—"

"No, sheriff, you listen. You have one lousy augment. That makes you mostly human, which makes you mostly weak. You are a target here and I'm going to have to protect you. Keep your coat on and keep your toys fully engaged. Keep an e-cuff available at all times in case we need a quick takedown."

"Yes, sir."

"Don't call me *sir*."

"Yes, miss."

"That's better."

We hovered over the place for ten minutes, trying to get a feel for it. Trish wanted to rush in but I had a feeling. It was the sort of feeling that a normal guy might call fear and a smart guy might call intuition. I called it a feeling in my gut. I made Trish order her car to float there for ten minutes so we could see what was coming and going.

The building was old. Most of the buildings here were old, but this thing was ancient. It was big and had dozens of doors. It might have been some sort of retail back in its heyday, but it had been converted into a processing center. It was an L-shaped building that was covered almost to the point of complete concealment by a vine I recognized as iron kudzu.

Iron kudzu is a lot like the regular sort. It grows fast—dangerously fast. It can cover a hill in a day and swallow a building and trees in a week. Some years ago, some idiot scientist decided to engineer a variety of kudzu that would hinder troops during the civil war. It worked.

Fortunately, that scientist didn't make the kudzu eat people. Unfortunately, it ate metal. Augmented soldiers fell to the stuff, getting trapped and sometimes strangled. Those of us who were unaugmented just passed right through. It was one more advantage for us naturals, but in the end even we couldn't handle it. The stuff got into the wild and still grows all over Texas.

Twice during our ten-minute wait, we saw freighters—massive air trains with ceramic plating and photoelectric arrays mounted in long Mohawks down their middles—land on the back side of the building. The rumbling bellows from the first freighter indicated that it was packed with cattle ready for slaughter. The second one was a tanker, and I would have bet my six-shooter and a week's salary it was full of milk. It landed in the short leg of the L-shaped building.

My sunglasses fed me a constant flow of information, most of which I ignored. It was useless stuff. It told me the history of the area, names and faces of people who lived here a hundred years ago, and road maps for the roads that had been swallowed by kudzu years ago. Like I said, useless.

"We go in down there." I pointed at the short leg of the building. "Where you can see that dead spot in the kudzu."

Trish bit her lip. "No way."

"We just need to get inside," I said. "And that's the best way."

"I'm not going anywhere near that stuff." There was a hint of actual fear in her eyes. I figured she had to be afraid of something, but I never would've guessed she'd let it show.

"My glasses tell me there are doors all along the side of the building. It used to be a shopping center, you know." Not so useless after all. I reached down and pulled out the bin that Trish had been organizing earlier. I rifled through the junk until I found what I needed: a four-inch, jet-black ceramic blade. I tested its sharpness with my thumb.

"You'll never get past those plants."

"We'll see about that. They'll never let us talk to the man in charge if we go in the front door."

She rolled her eyes, but I could tell she was going to cave. For a moment, just a brief moment, I didn't entirely dislike her.

"Tell you what, you wait out here and I'll give it a shot. If I'm not out in thirty minutes, you come right in the front door and get me."

"Pick up your corpse, you mean?" Trish concentrated for a second and the cruiser drifted over the patch of kudzu I had spotted earlier. "I'll glitch their surveillance as you drop down, I'm already giving them a blind spot for us, so it shouldn't be hard to hide your descent."

I smiled to myself. The thought of surveillance hadn't even occurred to me.

I leaned over the back of the cruiser and grabbed a tow cable with my left hand. The cable was black metal, just like my arm. It was incredibly thin and coiled in such a way that I could easily drop myself from the car fifty meters into the patch of dead kudzu. I stuck the ceramic blade between my teeth, gave Trish a salute, and dropped.

It was a perfect descent—fast, smooth, and right on target. I hit the center of the dead kudzu patch with just enough force to send my headache into fits and knives of pain through my knee.

The kudzu wasn't nearly as dead as I'd thought.

Like a coiled spring, the first vine I touched wrapped itself around my metal arm and pulled. I braced myself against it, but it had me unbalanced. My feet went out from under me and I fell forward.

It was all around me, choking out the hot sun and plunging me into darkness. Half a dozen long dead oaks scaffolded the kudzu, and I had landed only halfway down. I gasped at the depth of the patch. Farther down, the vine became woody—almost metallic. I grabbed the knife from my teeth and slashed at the vine that was holding my left arm.

I cut the vine just in time for another to spring into action. Iron kudzu wasn't any smarter than your average plant life. It only reacted to the movement of metal.

Below the top layer, vines were slower but stronger. I sprang out of the way of the next coil. My feet were unsteady on the springy vines below. My boots hadn't found soil, so I kicked off and dropped another few meters.

I almost made it.

A tendril shot down from above. Instinctively, I blocked with my right arm, but it didn't slow down. Sharp fire ran up my arm as the vine cut deeply into the back of my wrist. The jet-black blade fell to my feet as the wicked tendril wrapped around my shoulder.

The stiffened vines around me shuddered. They were getting closer. They'd squeeze the juice right out of me if I let them. I cursed modern science for about the millionth time and tried to pull free of the tendril.

It wasn't a lack of strength that stopped me. The tendril wasn't impossible to shake because it was strong. It was impossible because it was springy. No matter what direction I pulled in, the tendril just stretched and moved with me yet the resistance was enough that I couldn't escape.

I needed that knife.

Above, vines were wrapping around the black metal of Trish's tow cable. I let go of the cable, but it didn't ascend. I wondered if Trish would be able to pull free when she needed to get away.

The knife was at my feet. The tip had landed straight down and lodged in a thick vine. Once, twice, three times I kicked at it, trying to dislodge the knife. No luck. The tendril tightened. I could see marks in the metal where acidic sap was beginning to tarnish the polish.

The hardened vines were edging closer. I pulled hard at the tendril and edged a little to the left, where there was still some space. The open clearing was only a meter farther down, but it might as well have been a kilometer.

An offshoot of the tendril brushed the front of my coat.

"Whoa, miss. Not so frisky," I said. I batted it away.

It came back relentlessly. It was thin like a pen, but as it coiled it looked to me like it was trying to gently pick my pocket.

I smiled.

It was trying to pick my pocket, or coil around it in any case.

"Here, miss," I said. "I'll save you the effort."

Pulling against the vine that held my wrist, I dug deep into my pocket with my right hand and pulled out a fistful of little metal marbles. My e-cuffs, all of them, were attracting these vines and there wasn't anything I could do to stop them.

I tossed the cuffs up—as high as I could and as far. They mostly bounced off of the younger vines, but when they hit the older vines they stuck.

There was enough metal in the old vines that the things activated.

A black light surged into the back of my eyeballs. Next I knew, I was on the ground, face first in the red dirt. Not three meters from me was a crude stone door, complete with a carved wooden doorknob.

Above me, the vines were twitching and convulsing from the pulse of the e-cuffs. Vines lashed and spun for as far as I could see. I spotted the knife I'd lost in one, but it would be too dangerous to reach for it.

I crawled to the door. Every muscle in my body was sore, but I fought against it and reached up to the wooden knob. The door was unlocked. I slipped inside and pulled it closed behind me, waiting for my eyes to adjust to the darkness.

They didn't, but the sunglasses shifted quickly enough. A colorless image appeared before my eyes and I could see well enough. I was in.

Chapter 8

"You all right?" Her voice shot loud through my head, and I just about jumped out of my skin. It was Trish.

"The hell, woman?"

"The plants went all crazy down there. I thought maybe they'd killed you."

After a little silence, I replied, "If they'd killed me, they wouldn't be moving."

"Oh." I maybe detected some amusement in her voice. "They weren't moving for a while."

"They were killing me for a while." I forced myself to stand up and stretch the stiffness out of my legs. The pulse from the e-cuffs had not helped the various aches and pains that had followed me all day. "You might want to see if you can get that towline free, deputy."

"Will do, sheriff."

There was a doorway without a door on the far side of the room, an open maw that belched the mechanical noises and the acrid smoke of some unknown monstrosity. The room was a mess—a clutter of desks and debris. One wall looked to be a shrine to dead technology. A dozen generations of computers were piled in a haphazard array across the floor. Shelves held valuable-looking equipment. My guess was that this was all left over from the previous owners, and whether the latest owners were squatters or legitimate owners, they'd never bothered to sort through any of it.

As far as I could tell, there was only one thing of any real value in the entire room. A circle of chairs surrounded the center of the room. In the center of the circle was a small wooden table like the kind people used to own back when wood was an inexpensive building material. On that desk was something I hadn't seen in ages.

It was a bible, printed on paper and bound in leather. Long after digital took over the written word industry, the bible had survived. I had heard it said that the bible was the first book mass-produced by the printing press, and also the last. Those days were long gone, though. Nobody'd made them for years, which was why they were so valuable. I was looking at a collector's item.

I picked up the bible and leafed through its dangerously thin pages. I remembered those books from the days before the war. My mother had kept one at the bottom of an old trunk. It had been passed down through her family for generations. Conrad had found it once, and he wouldn't stop asking her what it was. Eventually, she gave in and said it was a dead relic from a dead religion, left to collect dust and not cause anybody any more harm. I wondered what had happened to that book. My best bet was that my father had long since sold or destroyed it. He never did go for such things.

The book in my hands had not been left to collect dust. That book was something someone used. From the gold foil on each page and etched leather binding, you could tell this was something someone really adored. It even smelled good, like leather and roses.

The sound of voices sent me ducking down behind the cover of the chairs. I was built for stealth about as good as one of Brown's longhorns, but I wasn't fixing to be found just yet.

"You get that latest shipment yet?" The voice was male—the sort of voice that always sounded like a whisper but carried the force of authority.

"Yes, señor." The second voice was strange. It was hard to place what was wrong with it, but having run into a good variety of weirdoes on the job, I was able to place it. "It arrived twenty minutes ago. We are processing it now, and distribution should go out later tonight."

"Is it the same as the others?"

"Yes."

"Good. We cannot afford another break in production."

The voices passed, so I hailed Trish. "Deputy, we have wikis down here."

"Shit." She was sounding less and less professional. "So much for cornering one of them."

Wikis were about as wrong as a person could get, as far as I was concerned. Take a perfectly decent human brain, then network it with a dozen other perfectly decent brains. Connect all of that through some neural uplinks to a central computer. That's a wiki. They are the absolute extreme of shared information, but I had never heard of them sharing emotional data, which gave them some very small, lingering sense of individual identity.

It was a wiki who took my arm in the war. Slowly, painfully, and surgically, it had removed my arm and carefully cauterized the wound. I never did know why it hadn't just killed me. It might have been some sort of new psychological warfare, designed in that twisted hive mind. If that was the case, it worked.

A cold sweat trickled down the back of my neck.

Bottom line: if one of them spotted me, they'd all know I was there. Trish was right. I couldn't corner one. Also, wikis tended to replace as much of their human bodies as possible. They could easily overpower me. If it came down to any sort of fight, I was not likely to get out of there alive.

Not that my odds were all that good to begin with.

"So, I suppose I'll be sneaking, then." I said.

"Good luck with that, boss." I sensed a little too much amusement in Trish's voice. "You want me to lay down a distraction?"

"Not yet."

I tossed the bible back onto the table and moved over to the doorway. The hallway was dark, lit only by dim red lights flickering high above. Just outside the door, a conveyor belt moved steel one-liter bottles from left to right. They were empty at that stage, but a machine was filling them a short distance down the line.

The wikis were a lost cause. I had to avoid them if I wanted to get out alive, but one of the many things I'd learned about wikis during the war was that they don't like to talk. Not only do they avoid vocalization, but they also don't even bother to properly form words among themselves.

That wiki in the hall had been talking. I needed to corner the guy he was talking to.

They had gone to the right, so that's the way I went too. My sunglasses had an echolocation feature, but the machinery in there was confusing it.

It wasn't hard at first. There was a wiki adjusting something on the bottling machine. I spotted his long, metallic neck and gangly arms quick enough that I was able to duck down behind a bottling machine before he turned my way. The yellow glow of its eyes pierced the dimly lit hallway, casting flickering shadows on the far wall.

Crouched, I started to move my way past. Did I say I was as sneaky as a longhorn? Make that a whole herd of them. Wearing cowboy boots was pretty much the same as wearing tap-dancing shoes and a cowbell.

Luckily, sneaking isn't always about being quiet. Good sneaking is about blending in. It's about being as much like the background as possible, in terms of sound, sight, and smell.

I sensed the wiki's movement on the other side of the console.

I froze.

My fingers touched the cold cement floor, and I strained my ears to sense any more movement.

The machinery continued its tumult of activity. The rhythmic thrum of the bottler almost drowned out the pounding of my heart.

I breathed slowly, matching the rhythm of the machine, not wanting to alert the ultra-sensitive ears of the wiki.

I took a step forward, then another. I matched the rhythm of my steps with the rapid metronome of the bottler.

Once I was past him, I stole a glance backward. The wiki's head was tilted, as if he knew something was wrong. He wasn't looking my way.

Ahead, I could see another open doorway into another junk-filled storeroom. Beyond that I could see a smaller doorway with an actual door. That was where I needed to be.

Matching my rhythm again with the machine, I made my way forward. The loudest sounds of the room faded behind me as I got closer to the door.

There were more noises coming from the room. Voices, muffled too much for my ears, rang out angrily. They were two voices—human, as far as I could tell. One of them might have been the smooth voice from before, but the other was definitely not a wiki. It had the defiant tone of youth.

The shades proved themselves useful once again. Yellow text started flying in front of my eyes, presumably translating the words that were being spoken behind the door. I moved back into a corner, where visibility to me would be reduced in case the wiki looked my way.

"God's work, Sammer." I thought that this must be Mr. Smooth. "People need this. We're saving people."

"I know it's God's work. We did everything just like normal."

"Yet, the law is involved?"

"Yeah. This morning..."

There was a gap in the conversation. It was still going on behind the door, but they must have shifted because the glasses could no longer pick up the words.

Back down the hall, machines continued to roar their rhythmic cacophony.

I edged forward to better catch the conversation.

"In God's work, there sometimes needs to be sacrifices."

"Yes, sir."

"Hundreds are being saved every day. If one falls so that hundreds may thrive, doesn't that make sense?"

"I suppose. But, I don't even know..." The yellow text stopped again, even though the talking continued behind the door. I grumbled in frustration and crouch-walked right up to the door. I would be completely visible to anybody in the hall, but the text started up again.

"Must be done, my friend. If someone was there, as you say, then they will describe what happened. This will lead the law directly to us, and even though our souls are clean we will suffer great setbacks. You must do as you must."

"But Ben wasn't—"

"Then who else?"

"I don't know."

"Then you must do as you must." There was a pause. "Go now with God's blessing."

Straining my hearing, I could sense a door opening and closing in the room. Whoever that kid was, he was leaving out a back door.

"You get all that, deputy?" I asked.

"Enough of it."

"He's leaving now. Get eyes on him. Take him down if you can."

Just then, emptiness filled the air. Silence.

Everything had stopped. Fighting my fear, I looked down the hall to see the shiny-headed long neck of the wiki I'd snuck past. His hand was on a big red button, and he was staring at me with glowing yellow eyes.

"You will stop." His voice had that wrongness about it still. The thing started walking toward me on stilt-like legs that clanged against the concrete with every step. Farther down the hall, I saw more movement.

I stood and tipped my hat to the metal monster.

"Could use that distraction now, Trish."

The door was locked. At least, it would have been considered locked for legal reasons regarding breaking and entering. It was not, however, locked in any meaningful way. I popped the doorknob out of the door with an easy black metal backhand and ducked through the door.

My visit was not expected. Mr. Smooth was leaning too far back in his chair to start with. Upon seeing me he overbalanced backward, but I believe it was the sudden screeching siren that made him fall. I only caught a glimpse of the man before he toppled back. Black hair, crusted over with style. Baby-blue suit with a slim Texas tie. This guy looked about as smooth as he'd sounded.

I wanted to arrest the bastard. I really did.

Unfortunately, I had more pressing concerns. The door burst open behind me, just as I reached the exit on the opposite side.

The metal man crouched through the door, lumbering and lurching like he was drunk. His eyes found me for just a second. As I passed through the door, I felt a wave of heat from behind.

Then I was free. The scorching sun beat down on me, but my shades compensated. A short path carved through the heart of the kudzu, giving me a straight shot to a small side-landing zone.

I ran hard. My ribs hurt. My head hurt. My knee hurt. Everything screamed out against what I was doing, but I ran anyway.

"Could," I gasped for breath, "use... a... pickup."

I raised my left arm. A second later, I was flying through the air. Trish was reeling me in like a tarpon from the gulf.

"Glad to be of service." She smirked as she reached over the edge and hauled me into the cruiser.

I nodded, a sign of deep appreciation that I'm not sure she got. "You get eyes on the kid?"

"He's fast but I'm tracking him. Speed he's going, we should be able to pick him up just past the wind wall."

"Good. I'm tired of this damn city."

She smiled at that. "You and me both, J.D."

Chapter 9

I wasn't one to sleep on the job—normally, that is.

It took a lot longer than expected to catch up to the punk biker. The kid's skidder was fast. With incredible maneuverability and some truly amazing acceleration, the kid managed to get out of the city a lot faster than I thought possible. Trish assured me that outside of the city we would have the advantage. I hoped it was true. She sent the cruiser up high and opened the throttle.

My head hurt. My back hurt. I felt old. I pushed tenderly at my ribs to see if anything was broken, but everything seemed like it was in place. The gash in my hand from the kudzu started oozing blood again, so I wrapped a bandage around it, wincing at the sting. My knee was swollen and I actually had to think for a minute before I remembered that the injury was from my fight with Jenkins.

The energy had left me. All that adrenaline just suddenly wore off. I put my feet up on the soft cushions of the cruiser and lay back while Trish stared out of the front of her vehicle like a cat ready to pounce on a spider. The top of the convertible was down, but an environmentally controlled bubble kept the wind from our faces.

I must have fallen asleep within seconds.

I'm a kid again. I have both of my arms. I'm waiting in the back of Pa's shiny new flying car, peering over the edge to a rusted-out old warehouse below.

I'm amazed at the way the car just floats there. It doesn't drift like our old bucket. The frame's forged out of some fancy new dark metal. I remember hearing someone say it was made out of black metal—the stuff they forge from dark matter and iron. Ma would hate it, like she hates all of the best toys. I turn to tell my little brother all about it.

He's not there.

Then I remember Conrad isn't ever going to be there. He's dead.

Gunshots ring out below. Each shot echoes a metallic pang against the old tin building. Each shot startles me just as much as the previous one.

My heart pounds and I gasp for breath. I duck down from the side of the car and curl up in the middle.

Then Pa's back in the car.

"What happened, Pa?" I ask.

"Justice, son" he grumbles. "Just some justice."

When I look up, Denise Brown is in the car. It's not the same car, though. It's Trish's cruiser and Denise is too close.

She leans even closer. Her soft body brushes against mine.

"You'll find them, won't you?" She whispers this into my ear like she's nibbling the words into place.

I nod.

"You gotta help me, sheriff," she whispers. Her breasts are heaving as she breathes, rubbing against me. "Help me get what I need."

I nod again, my body's responding to her advances, but something feels wrong.

She grabs my shirt and pulls me on top of her. She plants kisses on my neck and all over my collarbone.

Then I woke up.

Trish was looking at me. One corner of her mouth was turned up in that infuriating smile.

I blinked the sleep out of my eyes. "Ugh," I said. "That was messed up."

"Sounded like a perfectly normal dream for a young boy like yourself."

I shot her a look, realizing too late that she couldn't really see my eyes through my sunglasses. "Strange dream is all. Dreamed about Denise Brown."

"That's..." She seemed to search for an appropriate word. "An interesting choice."

"It is, but not really one I can imagine myself making. I'm not interested in lady folk, you know."

"Aw..." She smirked that annoying smirk again. "This isn't your desire to be the perfect traditional Texas cowboy rearing its head again, is it? Maybe your repressed heterosexuality is trying to break free in your dreams."

I pulled off my hat and scratched my head. "Even if I were into the ladies, I don't think Mrs. Brown would do it for me." I paused and considered what Trish had said. "And I don't have repressed sexuality."

"Sure you don't."

"Well—"

"I've seen how you look at Johnson when he's not paying attention."

I nodded. There was no use denying it.

"I've also seen how he looks at you."

I raised an eyebrow.

"I used to be a detective of sorts, J.D.," said Trish. "I'm observant."

"I suppose you are. We likely wouldn't be out here if you weren't, would we?" I meant it as a compliment. Justice was being served by our investigation and some good might have come from it.

She turned away. "If it's too much work, I can just drop you off at the station, you know."

"Too much work?"

"Weren't you planning on napping all day? Isn't that pretty much all you do?"

I felt my face get flushed—maybe from embarrassment, maybe from anger. "Just so you know, deputy, I do a hell of a lot out here. Just live outside the city a while and you'll see how the law doesn't mean what it used to. For Dead Oak, I'm the line between justice and chaos. The lawmen that are left are hardly more than flunkies following orders. Without me out here, people start making their own law. When people do that, you can bet it's just as good as no law at all."

"Even Johnson?"

"What?"

"Even Johnson is a flunkie?"

"Maybe. Truth is, I think he just follows orders. I don't think he gives a damn about me or the justice I keep."

"I suppose that could be true."

"Might be."

"What if the city took an interest again?"

"In Johnson?"

She narrowed her eyes. "What if Austin sent lawmen out to help you maintain order."

I stared at her. "Miss," I said, "that's just about the worst of all the options. Some of us fought hard for the rights of us outlanders. You city folk start sending your law out here and we might as well have lost that war."

"Didn't you?"

"It was a draw."

"Huh."

"Huh?"

"Doesn't seem like a draw."

"I'm glad you noticed. People around here don't think any of you city folk are even aware we're out here."

She looked down at the floor. "Most aren't. A few people in charge are starting to take more notice."

That didn't sound good to me. I started to wonder again just exactly why Trish had moved out of the city. I didn't ask, though. I figured my chances of getting a straight answer were pretty poor.

"Well," she said, "I'd love to continue this conversation, but we're closing in on that skidder."

"How long was I out, anyway?"

"'Bout ten minutes is all."

"Huh." I shook the grogginess from my head. Something felt wrong but there wasn't time to think on it.

I looked up and my glasses zoomed in on what looked like a speck in the distance. It was a kid on a skidder much like the one I'd encountered that morning. It left a trail of wispy black exhaust, and two impressive flames trailed behind it. He was flying low, hugging the Colorado Husk.

"Can you ground him?"

"Not without scattering him and his skidder over a kilometer of wasteland." She frowned and closed her eyes for a moment. "I can't seem to lock onto him. He must have a modded bike."

"No kidding."

It was pretty obvious that the bike was modded. They called those things skidders for a reason. They'd go so fast and were so likely to fail that if you rode one you were eventually going to end up skidded across the ground in a spectacular show of destruction. We didn't even bother to collect skidders when they went down. Animals take care of the human remains, and there weren't usually enough serviceable parts left to bother collecting the bike.

The blue flames were the first tipoff that this was a modded bike. Stock machines would usually forego the use of combustible fuels, but modded bikes often leaned toward dependence on old tech from a time before cheap, efficient gravity manipulation became popular. Some even used fossil fuels, despite the obvious inefficiencies. Based on his speed, it was something powerful. A shielded drive core would explain Trish's inability to bring it down nicely. I wondered what other modifications that thing had.

"Well," I said. "We could just follow it."

She frowned again. "No, I think I can bring it down."

I stood up to get a better view of the biker. A blast of hot wind threatened to take my hat, but I held it with my metal hand. My sunglasses zoomed in on the kid again. He kept quickly glancing back at us.

"Do it."

Trish lurched the cruiser forward, threatening to send me off balance. I kept my footing and we closed the distance in a matter of minutes.

"Just stay up here," Trish shouted. The wind was howling around us. At this speed, the protective bubble around the cruiser was starting to fail. Heat was seeping in, reminding me of how late in the day it was. Noon had come and gone while we were in Austin.

Trish pulled out her towline and clipped it to a hook that folded out from her waist.

The distance closed fast at first, then the blue flames flared and the skidder put up another burst of speed.

We were higher than he was and about fifty meters back. The tiny bike might have been hard to spot against the landscape, which was flying by at two hundred kilometers per hour. Ahead, I could see a field of onyx windmills blackening the skyline. If we reached it, this job would get a lot harder.

Forty meters. Then thirty. The cruiser shook beneath my feet, but still I stood. Most of the job was pure intimidation, and I'd be damned if I was going to back down. The kid kept glancing back at me nervously. Each time he did, his bike wavered a little in the air. He started to drop, leveling around fifteen meters above the broken landscape.

Twenty meters back, Trish moved to the hood of the cruiser. Wind whipped her hair and tore at her clothes. Unblinking, she focused on her prey.

Ten meters back. The biker swooped low and banked hard to the left, but the cruiser followed. It didn't turn as sharp, but it made the turn and closed the distance.

I lost sight of him as he vanished beneath the cruiser, but Trish's intense look told me he was still there.

Then she pounced.

She was fast—faster than any natural could be. I blinked and she dropped out of sight, the towline humming as it gave her more slack.

I heard the impact, but didn't see it. The towline, presumably under Trish's control, started reeling her in.

Holding onto my hat, I leaned over the side to make sure everything was going according to plan. Trish had the kid in a headlock, but he was struggling.

A scream pierced the air. At first I thought it might be the kid. Then I thought maybe it was Trish.

I leaned farther over the side to see what was happening. They weren't screaming.

It was the towline.

The device fought hard to reel in more line, but it was jammed.

"Aw, hell," I muttered.

I pulled the cover off of the reel and swore again. The towline had been tangled with a wad of kudzu. It had bound up completely. It was smoking.

"Land the cruiser!" I shouted over the side. I didn't know if she'd heard me, but the cruiser didn't slow down. I wondered how I could transmit to her like I had back at the processing plant.

The skidder jerked to one side, then the other. The fight was still going on down there, and I couldn't tell who was winning.

I moved to the backseat, where I'd spotted the manual controls earlier. I pulled the cover off so that I could get a good look at the array of blinking, unlabeled buttons. It was enough to make me swear a third time.

I needed a new plan.

Trish was only about fifteen meters out. We were lower. At about ten meters from the ground, we were almost even with the biker. We were going too fast. Hot winds threatened my hat again, but this time I took it off and stuffed it under the seat.

A lawman doesn't have many tools. Justice is a funny thing that way. Sometimes all it took were fists or words.

But, sometimes it took a gun.

I pulled out my six-shooter. It was heavy in my hand and felt good. It was warm.

Steadied against the side of the cruiser, I drew a bead on the two of them struggling on the skidder. Blue flames blinded me for a second, but I blinked it off.

I didn't worry about hitting Trish. She was pretty much bulletproof. The bike was packed full of explosive fuel, as far as I knew, so I had to avoid hitting it.

They lurched to the side again. We were closing in on the windmill field. This needed to be resolved soon or it was going to get a lot more dangerous.

There was no room for hesitation. I needed to disable the kid.

When Trish pulled him hard to one side, I shot at his head.

Even with bulletproof skin and a reinforced skull, a bullet to the head would scramble his brains pretty good.

The kid flinched at just the wrong second. Somewhere far below, I shot up some quality Texas soil that didn't even have it coming.

Trish took advantage of the opportunity. She pounded her fist into the back of the kid's skull. He went limp. She grabbed control of the bike. The skidder and cruiser, now both under her control, simultaneously slowed and dropped. They landed just in front of the first towering black windmill.

I grabbed my hat and hopped out of the cruiser.

Trish heaved the kid off of the bike and slammed him onto the ground.

"Well done, deputy," I said.

She glared at me. "What the hell happened up there?"

"Towline jammed. I told you to make sure the kudzu was cleared off."

"You never said that."

"Meant to."

The kid let out a moan and shifted. Trish smashed his face into the ground with the heel of her shoe. "Fucker put up more of a fight than I thought he would. Has a death wish or something." I'd never seen her so mad.

"Yeah, something's up with this kid."

Trish scrunched her nose at me. "Kid? J.D, this guy is in his twenties. He's not a kid."

There was silence while I sauntered around the skidder and the guy who'd been riding it. The blue flames weren't just exhaust from the engine. They were an overall theme. Stylized electric blue flames were painted across the body of the vehicle and tattooed all over the kid's arms. On the back of his leather jacket, two hammers were crossed in an X.

"There's a point in life where a person looks around him and starts to take some responsibility." I pulled out a wad of snuff and slowly inserted it behind my lip. "Not just for his own actions, but for all the shit that goes on around him. This kid isn't there yet—not by what I've seen."

My slow circling around the kid brought me back to Trish. When I was next to her, I reached my metal hand around her hip and pulled her close. Her eyes got wide but then narrowed when she felt me unclip the towline from her waist. I followed the line back to the cruiser, coiling it like a lasso as I walked. Once I was close to the cruiser, I grabbed the line and pulled hard with my right arm while positioning my left in just the right way. I got the line into a tiny cutting tool and snipped it off.

The kid was starting to move again. I lashed the line around his wrists, pulling them back hard. Then I ran the line back to his ankles and tied him up in just about the most uncomfortable pose possible. I pulled each knot hard, giving him as little freedom as possible, in case he had some artificial double joints. It probably wouldn't matter, but I would have hated to give the kid the idea that he might get away.

"You know, I have cuffs if you need them." Trish was shuffling her feet uncomfortably, watching as I quietly tied the kid.

"Lawman who can't hogtie his own criminal ain't much of a lawman, now, is he?"

From the kid, I ran the cable four meters to his bike. I tied it, making sure it didn't have any play. There's a trick to getting metal ropes like that to bind properly when you tie them in knots, and I knew what I was doing. The kid wasn't going anywhere.

The controls on the bike were pretty straightforward. I powered the system up and found a button that lit the afterburners.

The wave of heat shocked the kid out of his beauty sleep.

"What the—"

"Watch the language son," I grumbled at him. "We've got a lady present."

"Fuck!" The kid wasn't in the listening mood.

"Look, son," I spat a stream of brown chew. "I'm just looking to have that talk we never got to have at the Goat this morning."

The kid's eyes got wide.

"You ran for a reason, didn't you? Pretty clever to have your friend bait me while you ducked out the back door. Even better to have your other buddy come back to pick up the bait. Nobody got caught and nobody was around to point fingers at you."

He smiled but I could see that he was straining against the towline.

"It's black metal, son. Not likely you'll break that. Might cut it if you have the right tool."

I waited while he discovered that truth on his own. He was stubborn, so I gave him some credit.

"So, I just have a few questions."

The kid kept struggling. Turned out he did have a few double joints. If he hadn't been properly hogtied, he might have been able to rotate his arms all the way around in front of him.

My glasses finally got a good read on the kid's face, the screen flashed a name and address.

"Little Sammy Clevins," I said, slowly. "I knew your mother back in the day." She had been an addict, ruined by men and drugs. I'd helped her get into rehab about a dozen times, but I wasn't sure it ever took.

Sam looked like he was testing out a theory that he could glare me to death.

"Got yourself in a bit of trouble, Sam." I leaned casually against his bike. It was a damn fine skidder. I ran my finger along its graceful curves and admired the immaculate paint job. "Now, the good government of Texas doesn't much care what you do with your spare time, but there are still a few things you and I both know are illegal. How about you just give me a list of what you might be up to these days and I'll let you know what concerns me."

The kid continued his silence. Behind him, waves of hot Texas air were making the sea of windmills dance. It was thirsty weather. In more ways than one, I needed a drink.

I flipped a switch and a belch of blue flame rolled out in the kid's direction. The bike lurched forward a few meters, dragging the kid with it. I walked casually to where the bike had landed, and I turned to face the kid.

"So," I said. "Questions?"

He glared at me. His left eyebrow let up a little wisp of smoke. Apparently, blue flames are pretty hot.

"You know anything about that Daniel Brown fella? Guy who was killed last night?"

"I don't—" I reached for the switch again. "Sorry. I mean, yeah. I've met him. I didn't kill him, if that's what you're thinking! Jesus, what the—"

I flipped the switch. The kid turned fast enough that most of the heat just scorched the back of his jacket.

"What the hell do you want? That fucking hurts!" He was grasping at a higher octave.

"I'm sorry, son. I guess I thought I heard some bullshit. I'm sure it won't happen again." I found a dial on the control panel and clicked it up a notch. I guessed that the dial would up the fuel that vented into the engine, causing a bigger burst. The whites of the kid's eyes told me I was probably right.

"Sheriff." Trish's voice was barely audible compared to the roar of the two skidder engines. "I'm pretty sure torture's against the protocol. Don't you think?"

I narrowed my eyes at her and she backed down. There was no protocol that far out in the wild. The fact that she didn't know that just reinforced her status as a shiny-headed city girl.

"Boy." I brought out my best scowl. "You'd best be telling me everything you know."

The kid had the audacity to throw a pleading look Trish's way. I reached for the switch.

"No, wait!" He winced, cowered on the ground, and tried to inchworm his way as far from the bike as possible. "I'll talk. *Pinche culero.* I'll talk. I didn't kill the guy. I don't know who did, all right." His voice was about as high as I expected it to be in this situation.

"All right," I backed away from the button. "Talk."

"Bunch of us got a call to go talk to the guy about some business. We found him at the bar, got him out back, and had a little discussion. A rough one." He cleared his throat. "That's it, man. That's the last I saw him."

"Your buddies find him later? Maybe finish the job?"

"No, man. Well, maybe. I stayed at the Goat. Sucked down some cold ones and headed home when that fuckin' preacher man showed up and started giving everyone a hard time."

"What preacher?"

"I don't know, *pendejo.* Just some fucker who likes to bug anyone who's havin' a good time. He's trouble, you know? There's just something wrong with the guy."

"Why not rough him up a little too?"

Sam bit his lip. His eyes searched the horizon. "Dude always has backup, you know. Always lookin' to baptize someone whether they want it or not. Couple of my guys got into some bad shit with them."

I couldn't think of any reason to care about some religious wacko trying to forcibly convert a bunch of unrepentant gangsters. The idea amused me, actually. "So, who sent you to rough up Mr. Brown?"

The kid hesitated again. All I needed to do was look at the switch. "The guy calls us sometimes. He's in the food business. Guy's name is Billy Sharpe. Dude's a real *chingada madre*."

"I bet. The guy you were talking to in Tarrytown?"

He nodded.

"He's in charge of that operation?"

"Yeah."

I figured I would follow up on that another day. Food distribution and all of its regulations didn't really concern me. I still wasn't convinced it had anything to do with the murder.

"So, that's it, man. That's all I know." Sam swallowed. "You gonna let me go?"

I glanced at Trish. She was biting her lip.

"Yup," I said.

"What?" Trish's jaw dropped.

I untied the line from the skidder and gave the loose end to Trish. "If there's one thing I'm decent at, it's tellin' what a man is capable of. I can tell you pretty close to how high a person can jump. I can tell how far a person can walk in the desert before they drop, and I can tell you whether or not a person's going to be able to kill a man one day and lie about it the next."

I gave the kid a good scowl, then a nice toothy grin.

"This kid doesn't have what it takes to kill a man."

Trish leaned in close and spoke so the kid couldn't hear. "He was going to kill Ben Brown. We heard him talking to his boss about it."

"Well, I suppose that's something he may have intended to do," I rumbled in a voice nearly as quiet as hers. "But he hasn't done it yet, has he?"

"No."

"Then we'd best be on our way." I turned to the kid. "Son, you head east about twenty kilometers and you'll find the Brown Ranch. Just follow that there line of mills."

"What?"

"You heard me, kid. If ya feel too guilty of something you've done or something you were gonna do, then just wait here. I'll have a cruiser pick you up in a few hours."

The kid's eyes wandered to his skidder.

"I'll be confiscating that. I suspect it's been used in a crime, so we gotta work it over some—see if there's evidence on it."

He slumped. The kid was beat.

"Well, deputy." I swung a leg over the bike and scanned the controls to make sure I knew what I was doing. "Meet me at the Brown Ranch. I believe we have some business to take care of."

Without bothering to wait for Trish to move the poor bastard, I kicked into the air. That beautiful machine took off like a rocket, complete with a deafening roar and searing fireball. The scorching Texas afternoon air scoured my face and nearly took off my hat. There was no environmentally controlled bubble around this thing. I wondered how that kid managed to go as fast as he did.

It didn't matter, though. Something had been bothering me since that morning, and Sam's little mission confirmed it. Ben had seen something that night. I didn't think it was true when he'd tried to tell me that morning, but now it had just about gotten him killed. I wondered how it might have played out if I hadn't been there to stop Sam.

I wondered how it would play out now that I had.

Times were rough out there around Dead Oak, and sometimes I was the only justice people got a chance to see. Sometimes I wondered if there was any justice at all.

Chapter 10

Twenty minutes later, we were basking in the aroma of a rancher's late afternoon siesta feast in the Brown's cramped kitchen.

I glanced around the table. Ma Brown's kids were there—at least most of them. There were twin girls, whose names I didn't remember. They looked to be about eight or nine. Ben, in all spikes and leather, was in the unfortunate position of being right in between the two pink-clad girls, caught in the crossfire of their too-loud whispers and shrill giggling. He didn't seem to care. He appeared to be more interested in glaring at me and sneaking glances at Trish. The kid Francis sat with a slack jaw while lights flashed in his eyes. Far as I could tell, he never once looked at anyone. Next to him was a high chair with a fat baby strapped into it and then there was Denise. Next to Denise, Trish sitting rigid in her seat with a look of mild disgust on her face. There were two other boys, maybe three and four, who sat quietly and stared at the food. They were the only two behaving like their father had been killed just that morning.

A whole pile of sausage-filled kolaches filled the center of the table. Forming a circle around it was a slew of grits, bacon, some fried eggs, and a huge loaf of steaming hot bread. A bowl of chopped fruit sat next to my right elbow on the thick slab of a table. Across from me was a pile of tamales, steaming and filling the air with peppery spices.

We weren't eating yet. Denise Brown was leading a silent grace, which was lasting far longer than I thought it should. My head still hurt, along with some stiffness from bruising that I could feel setting into various parts of my abused body. Stopping the hectic pace just seemed to let these aches sink in. I couldn't remember when I had last eaten. The empty pit of my stomach was calling out for those tamales, and I wasn't sure I could wait until the end of some damn long prayer to some god who didn't even exist.

Then, I felt something.

Deep behind my chest I felt something welling up. There was a constriction, like a difficulty pulling breath, but I was breathing just fine. My eyes watered and my chin quivered. I gripped the slab table with my right arm and squeezed hard. A tear ran down my cheek.

"Amen!" Ma Brown shouted the word, startling me.

"Amen," I said, not sure exactly why I felt the need to. I grabbed a kolache. The pastry pulled apart and a wave of steam wafted out of it, mixing with the spicy aroma of the hot tamales. I bit into it and did my best to savor it as the heat and spice slid down into the empty pit of my belly. Trish busied herself pushing some cubes of fruit around her plate like some sort of damn princess.

"Mighty fine meal you have here, ma'am," I said.

Ma Brown smiled. Her eyes gleamed and she shifted her metallic neck. "Well, we like to eat pretty good out here on this ranch, Mr. Crow. Glad you could come back out. I thought we might have gotten off a little bad this morning."

I nodded and continued to eat. The tamales made their way around, and I had to try one. I untied the string and carefully peeled back the cornhusk. A blast of the spicy steam rolled up around my face and I breathed it in. It was absolutely wonderful.

Ben finally caught Trish's eye. They locked gazes for a second. Trish ended up being the one who broke away. She had a scowl on her face. The kid grinned.

Denise seemed not to notice. "What are you here for, sheriff?"

"Besides the finest cooking this side of the Rio Grande?"

Her lips pulled into a smile, but her eyes were all business.

"Well, I do have some business here. Nothing to worry about, really."

"What kinda business?" He voice was cold.

"Ran into a boy just a ways away from here. Sounded like he might have meant your kid Ben some harm."

Trish jerked away from something under the table. It wasn't enough of a movement to cause a ruckus, but she frowned and sat with her feet at an awkward angle. Ben smiled but kept his eyes on his food.

"Nothin' to worry about?" Ma Brown asked.

"Well, ma'am, I don't believe he was going to go through with it. In fact, I believe it's someone Ben might already know."

Ben perked up and then went back to his food.

"Ben," I said, "you know a guy named Sam, right?"

"No."

"Let me reword that." I cleared my throat. "Ben, you know a guy named Sam."

He looked at his food like there might be a clever answer hidden there.

"Sammer the Hammer, you call him."

Ben smiled but didn't look up. "I know Sammer the Hammer," he said to his food.

I took a fried egg and slathered it with salsa. "Any idea why he might be headed this way to visit you?"

Ben was silent. He looked to Trish but she avoided his gaze.

I continued. "There's some who think he's coming to kill you."

He looked up at me now, briefly showing a worried look. I was worried too, though. I didn't know why I was so worried. I figured it was gut instinct to feel protective of the kid, like some paternal impulse was kicking in.

"Kid, I'd like to get you under some protection until this blows over."

"What?" His jaw dropped and he stood up. "Hell no! I'm safe right here."

I raised an eyebrow at him and took a bite of egg. I chased it with a glass of cool milk.

"Sammer wasn't on his way to kill me," Ben said, sitting back down. "He called me when he left Austin. Warned me that the boss was gunnin' for me. I told him it ain't nothin' to me. Bring it on."

"The boss? You work for Billy Sharpe?"

Ben gave the slightest nod. "Sort of."

"Sam warned you? Told you what Sharpe said?"

"Yeah, and he was going to pick me up, so we could get somewhere safe."

I glanced at Trish. Reading her expression was about as easy as reading a slab of granite.

"There might be more after you."

Ma Brown cleared her throat loudly. I realized then that she hadn't been eating. She was winning a contest for the best glare of the day.

"Sheriff Crow," she said deliberately. "Would you care to explain to me exactly what this is about?"

"Certainly, ma'am." I finished my egg and sopped up the yolk with a hunk of bread. "Well, for starters we believe your husband may have been murdered."

"He was murdered," Trish interrupted. "We're sure of it."

"He was murdered, but we're still tracking down the killer—"

"Well, you should have just asked," she interrupted. "It was them damn Cinco Armas. They always comin' out here, givin' us hard time."

Ben got a serious interest in his food.

"Well," I said. "They're under consideration, but we want to make sure we're doin' things right. You know much about the business side of this here ranch?"

"For instance," added the deputy, "do you know who you work with for the distribution of your dairy?"

It was Ma Brown's turn to gain a profound interest in her plate. "Dan took care of all that. Wasn't no need for me to get into it."

Trish kept pressing. "So you don't know about him getting dropped from the three major distributers?"

Denise shook her head without looking up from her plate.

"Well, we think there might have been an issue with the milk—a contamination issue. Know anything about that?"

Ma Brown knit her eyebrows together in anger. I felt it too. Trish had no right to treat a murder victim's wife with such rudeness. It was insensitive—maybe even cruel. To attack the product of Ma Brown's ranch was the deepest kind of insult.

"Trish," I said in a low growl. "Back off a little."

"No, I don't need to back off a little. This is important. We need this information, J.D."

"But we don't need it right now. We don't need to get it here."

Ma Brown let out a sob.

"J.D, listen. We need to track down this killer as soon as possible before the leads dry up. This is how I used to do it back in Austin, and I don't see why it can't work out here."

I wiped the corners of my mouth and put the napkin on my plate. "Out here things work a little different. You know that already."

She leaned in close and whispered, "How could she not know this stuff?"

I spoke back in a calm voice for everyone to hear. "We stick a little closer to tradition out here, deputy. The wife's role is labor and tech. She manages the physical side of the operation. Man's role is traditionally money business and keeping the house clean. Raising the kids. That sort of stuff." It came out a little more hard line than I meant it. "Look, I understand that's not what you're used to in the city, but that's how it goes out here."

Trish stood up. "All right," she said. "I think I'm done here. You want me to go pick up that Sam kid?"

"Might as well. If he's on his way here, go ahead and give him a ride home. If he's where we left him, send him to lockup."

"You were serious about that then?"

I gave her a dry look.

"Right," she said.

I met her gaze for a moment, trying to figure out what was going on in her head. When that didn't work, I tapped my ear, indicating she should keep our audio link open. She nodded but didn't look happy.

Trish thanked Ma Brown and smiled at the kids. She didn't get much love back, but the nod was probably more than she deserved. She showed herself out. A moment later, I heard the deep hum of her cruiser lifting off.

I leaned back in my chair and picked at my teeth with a toothpick. A fat, lazy fly buzzed around the room. I watched it move from ceiling to food then back to ceiling again. The kids ate in silence, but Denise Brown didn't seem to have an appetite.

"'Preciate the meal, ma'am," I said once the kids had nearly finished.

She smiled at me. "Any time, Mr. Crow."

She meant it too. Thing about tradition is that sometimes it opens just as many doors as it closes. Tradition says that if a man comes to your house at mealtime, you feed him, especially if he's a man of the cloth or the law. Somehow that tradition still held strong, even though there weren't many of either type of man left. It was a good thing too. If not for tradition, I'd have still been hungry that day.

Ben spoke up. "If I come with you, will your deputy be in charge of my safety?"

"No." Trish's voice was in my ear immediately.

"Maybe," I replied.

He smiled.

When I had said the thing about taking Ben into custody, I had been completely serious. Standing out in the oppressive Texas heat next to that dangerous-looking blue flamed skidder, I wasn't so sure that having him along would really make him safer. Who could protect the kid better than his family? His mother certainly had some skill with the tech. She was likely a decent shot with a gun too. I didn't know whether the kid would be safer with me. Even if he was safer, it probably wasn't my place to take him away from his ma.

Still, he came. His mother stayed inside the house and tried to bore holes into my skull with her stare. Ben slouched his way out of the house. His hair was still spiked tall and black leather was covering every inch of his body except for his face. His eyes flashed red at me in the early afternoon sun. As far as I could tell, he hadn't brought anything with him, other than the clothes on his back.

We had just launched into the scorching Texas sky when Trish's voice came in through our audio link.

"J.D, you're going to want to come check this out," she said.

"What?"

"It's Sammer the Hammer." There was a long pause. "He's dead."

Chapter 11

"Johnson." I called the station once I'd scanned the body. "We got a body comin' in."

"Yes, sir." Johnson sounded tense, like he wasn't having so hot a day either. "Someone's looking for you, sir."

"Who?"

"Not sure. Some guy just came in ten minutes ago. Says he wants to talk to you before moving forward with something."

"With what?"

"No idea. Seemed to think he was in charge, though."

"What's he look like?"

"Pretty good-lookin' guy, dressed in black. Wouldn't tell me his name. Looks like some shiny from the city. Lot of metal, you know? Classy."

"I hear ya." I looked back at the body. "If he bothers you again, tell him I'm busy today. I'll talk to him when I damn well please."

Johnson hesitated, but then, "Yes, sir."

I felt a little guilty for making Johnson's day harder. I was guessing the man in black wouldn't give up so easily. This play would at least buy me some time, though. I was busy. By the look of it, I was getting busier.

Sammer the Hammer had been murdered. There was absolutely no doubt about it. He was about twenty minutes west of where we left him. The kid had passed my clever little guilt test. It wasn't proof of his innocence, but it was about as good as we were ever going to get.

He'd seen it coming. With my face right down close to the red earth, I could see in his footprints where he turned and leaned back. Something had approached him from the sky. The ground was harder near the windmill, but the scrubby grass was disturbed in more than one place. Some of it had been stepped on.

My breathing slowed down. I scanned the ground—not with some fancy computer, but with my eyeballs. I looked at the earth the way my mother had once taught me when I was very young, before she left. Back and forth, I took in all of the details of the landscape. To the untrained eye, there might not be anything to see, but I had spent years studying the effects of people and animals on the world. To someone like me, this land was full of information.

I pushed a tuft of brittle grass to the side with the toe of my boot. Beneath it was the first bullet hole, tiny and sunken into the earth. Trish started to work on it while I continued following the trail.

Closer to the jet-black windmill, things got a little more interesting. Sam had been running. His stride showed that pretty clearly. He kept turning back, twisting the ground as he did. He stumbled at one point, making a print with three fingers of his left hand in the sand. Something had been chasing him down hard, and I suspected that he knew whoever it was wasn't going to let him live.

There was dust on the mill. Normally, windmills get dusty. Windstorms toss up a lot of fine sand into the air and it settles everywhere. This leaves a certain pattern of dust. When it rains, the raindrops carry the dust and shift it around. This leaves a different pattern.

The dust pattern on this windmill was a third kind. It was reminiscent of a wind pattern that pointed up. The tracks closer to the windmill were muted, almost completely erased.

"Looks like we're looking for a mid-sized, air-handled vehicle, probably a car," I paused to glance at Trish. I needed to make sure she was listening. "No jets. Probably a darker color."

"How do you know?" She walked over, trampling the trail I'd just been through.

"Well, based on the size of this blowback on the mill and the center of the flattened area, we can pretty easily say this was mid-sized. It wasn't a skidder and it wasn't a freighter."

"Narrows it down."

"Vehicles that are air-handled use cold air blowers to fine-tune balance and speed. No burned grasses or glassed sand means there probably weren't any hot jets. This pattern of blown sand here shows where the vehicle maneuvered around the mill, chasing after the victim."

"So, why do you think it's a dark color?"

I walked slowly around the mill. My eyes fell on Sam again and I suppressed a shudder. I rubbed the bridge of my nose. The headache was coming back. I should have seen it coming. It was my fault that another innocent life was gone.

"Killers love dark colors," I said. "Black. Dark blue. Or red. It could be red."

She sighed and went back to scanning the bullet.

"Probably black," I said.

Somebody had completely ruined Sam. I figured Trish could probably spend a week sorting through all the bullet holes in Sam and the surrounding landscape. There'd been nowhere left for him to run. The tracks showed that he'd turned around, putting his left palm on the windmill. It was hot, so he'd immediately taken it off. The distraction had been enough, though, and the murderer had drifted around the corner on his flying metal steed.

The first shot had probably taken Sam in the torso. It had thrown him back, away from the mill—sprawled him out. The rest of the shots came while he was lying on the ground. His face was a pulp. His torso and arms were misshapen and clothed in the tattered remnants of his leathers. His bulletproof skin was torn to shreds. It takes a fast bullet or a heavy bullet to get through tweaked skin.

Yet Trish's scan showed there weren't any bullets in or around the body.

"I'll be damned," Trish said from around the side of the mill.

"What?" I said after a long enough pause.

"Black metal slivers."

"What?"

"Black metal. You're familiar?" She walked around the corner, holding a tiny sliver of metal between her fingers. "Military-grade, dark-matter-forged steel. In bullet form, sort of."

I squinted at the sliver of metal. It was black metal all right. Same dull shine as my left arm.

"This explains why Sam's skin didn't help him against the bullets." Trish bagged the sliver of metal. "These things are sharp and extremely hard. They'd pass right through most steel armor. Skin is nothing. In fact, the resistance created by armored skin actually significantly increased the damage done as this little needle passes through the body. I'd say he was probably only shot seven or eight times."

"Seven or eight?" I looked at the ruined corpse and had to wonder how so few bullets could've done that sort of damage.

"Yeah. Maybe nine." Trish eyed the corpse for another moment. "Black needles have an ugly effect on armored skin. The resistance upon impact creates enormous amounts of heat, leading to a sort of super-heated mini explosion. Messy, but very effective."

"Puts us in a whole new league."

"No kidding."

"Bullets this expensive have to be a professional's work."

Trish fell silent for a moment. "Could be someone from the city. Or military."

"Yet, there's some hate here." I nodded to the body. "You don't pump a body full of gold bullets just for fun. It's gotta mean something on a personal level."

"It's not like they left the bullets. The killer must have had some way to pick them all up quickly. That's why there aren't any bullets near the body."

"That the only one you found?"

"Yeah."

"I guess that's a break then. He must have had trouble finding that one."

Johnson's team would pick up the body. There was nothing left for us there. Trish and I headed over to her cruiser, where Ben was chained to a metal ring set into the passenger seat. Trish had protested, but I didn't want the kid contaminating the place before we got a decent take on it.

The kid was not happy about that.

"'Bout fucking time."

"Son, your friend's dead. Show some goddamn respect."

"Yeah, Sam's dead. What the hell did you do to stop that? You gonna protect me too? Big strong sheriff. What the hell?"

The kid went on like that for a while. He bothered me. It rankled me the way he was going on, disrespectful of the dead body not fifty meters from that spot. I was careful not to let it show, though. I'd never let the kid see that it bothered me.

I clicked open his cuffs so he could move around more easily. He hopped out of the cruiser and brushed past me. His little eleven-year-old feet stomped right around the windmill and then stopped.

Trish was still over there, so she moved next to him, crouched down, and put an arm around his shoulder. I didn't know what she said to him. I didn't know what I would have said. Right there was a kid whose world was falling apart. His pa was dead. The world of bravado and mutual bullying and posturing had been his crutch when his dad had died, and we'd just kicked it out from under him. Ben shifted and I could see the sheen of tears on his cheeks.

The truth was, kids scared the hell out of me. They were unpredictable and selfish. They didn't make any sense most of the time, except for when they did. Sometimes they made sense in a way that reminded you what's really important. That was worse, really.

The kid's world was crashing down around him. For just a moment, all of his posturing was stripped away and I could see the little boy behind it.

Then it was all back again.

"What the hell?" Trish shouted. She forcibly pulled Ben's hand off of her ass with one hand and then grabbed a handful of his leather jacket in the other. She lifted him up off the ground with one hand, keeping him at arm's length. "Listen, you little fuck. You try anything again, I will ship you to the flood plains for a decade of hard labor."

Trish stomped over to the cruiser, locking gazes with the kid the whole way.

"J.D?"

"Yup."

"So sexy," said the kid. "I just want to get on top of that. You might be the love of my life, babe. You know you wanna go home with me." His impish grin said that he was entirely unaware of how close he was to getting hit.

"You still want this?" Trish said.

I looked at the kid for a long moment. My plan had been to have Trish keep an eye on him while I scoped the old junction.

The kid was staring at her chest now, not even being subtle about it. "Mm, this is it, babe. You know you wanna be with me."

"Yup," I said.

"Then here you go." She dropped Ben on the ground, glared at me, and hopped into her cruiser. "You need anything else here, boss?"

"I don't suppose I do."

Without another word, she launched into the air and sped off. I imagined she was headed for the station. As independent as she was, I was fairly certain she would come up with some decent leads for the latest murder. After all, if anybody around here had a chance of tracking down a professional killer from the city, it would be her.

"What the hell is wrong with you, boy?"

Ben pulled himself to his feet and brushed the dust off of his leathers. "I'm precocious."

"Shut the hell up." I looked him over. "Look, you can come with me, but only if you help."

"Where we going?"

"You're Cinco Armas, right?"

The kid didn't say anything. I started walking to the skidder, which was parked a dozen meters away.

Finally, he said, "Yeah." The kid followed me. "Pa didn't like it."

"I bet."

"That ain't what got him killed, though."

"What makes you so sure? You didn't see anything, did you?"

He paused. "Not really. But it wasn't them."

"Were you at the Goat when your pa showed up?" I rifled through the saddlebags that were strapped to the skidder. When I found some cigarettes, I pulled two of them out of the pack and lit one. I handed the other to Ben.

"Yeah." He stuck the cigarette in his mouth and somehow lit it by snapping. "I mean, no. Not really. He was there when we got there. He was with some woman, so he didn't see me. I ducked out right away."

"So, you didn't know that Sam was going there just to find your pa?"

He sucked in the smoke like someone trying to prove that he was good at it. Good at smoking. Like that's a thing.

"No, I didn't." He looked down at his feet. "I guess there might've been a lot that went on that I didn't know."

"Suppose there probably was." I half sat on the bike and watched waves of heat ripple the air, making the windmills in the distance dance. The heat just seemed to cling to everything. Mills all around were buzzing fast. The wind had definitely picked up since the morning. "Who would you say I need to talk to for some answers?"

"Nobody, old man."

I scowled at the kid. "Who else?"

He ignored me and watched the mills spin for a while. Then, "Court."

"Court's gang all work for Sharpe?"

"Not all of them. It's just some extra on the side."

"You ever do anything for him?"

Ben bit his lip.

"You think Court will be at the Old Junction this time of day?"

He met my gaze but didn't say anything. I couldn't tell if he was afraid to rat out his friends or just shocked that I knew so much. Either way, I was a little surprised that the dentist's tip was going to pay off.

"I'm going to the Junction now. Should get there around dusk."

The kid dropped his cigarette.

"I'm not asking," I said. "I'm going whether you help or not."

"You're a fucking dead man."

"You think you can call them off enough so I can talk to this Court?" I stepped on his cigarette to put it out and leaned right down into his face. I spoke in a low voice. "I don't give a shit about what they got going on that's illegal," This was a lie, but I was willing to set things aside for a while, "All I want is a better timeline for last night. I got a feeling someone other than your little playmates followed your pa home."

"What makes you think it was someone else? Psychic powers?"

"Sam was convinced it was someone else. You seem convinced, or you wouldn't be so eager to please them still. That counts for about as much as a pair of twos in my book, but that and a bluff might be all I got to win this hand."

"Sounds to me like you're not too good at your job."

"I'm pretty decent at tossing mouthy kids into lockup."

"Not from what I've seen."

"You got a choice, kid."

The kid shifted back and forth a few times. He looked at Sam's skidder. Then he nervously glanced back to the mill where Sam's body lay mangled. "I'll get you a meeting with Court, but we gotta do it my way."

Like I said: unpredictable.

Or maybe I should've been able to predict that. Like I said before, I was no good with kids.

Chapter 12

The Old Junction was a relic of the past. It was a broken-down tower designed and built for a time when power was wired between the good people of Texas. Conduits ran into this junction point from the surrounding power sources. Back before the new junction was built, every windmill for a couple hundred kilometers shipped volts here. In turn, lines ran from here to the surrounding communities. The small towns and the ranches all got a share. As long as somebody was still sucking power out of the sky, everyone had a piece. The system was designed for sharing and stability and an open marketplace.

War changed all that. The New Junction across town had lines running from the ranches, just like this one. The difference was that the only lines running out of that junction lead straight to the city. If there's one thing those city-dwelling metalheads like, it's their volts. In return, they let us scrape out an existence out here in the waste.

The history books all say the Texas Civil War was fought to a draw. Some folks have a different opinion.

I crouched in my hiding spot, cursing myself for letting the kid dictate the terms of our agreement. I watched as the sun set behind the black two-story tower that was the Old Junction. Wind whipped across the broken ground, pulling sand and weeds up to dance around the jagged, angular building. Old architecture loved angles, and so did the wind. All the real business here was underground. The lines that were above ground had long since been harvested for metal or destroyed by storms.

The heat of the day had started to pass. The structure creaked and groaned as it cooled. The air was still hot, thick, and uncomfortable. My lungs struggled to pull it in. The air tasted of the oncoming storm. I didn't know how much time we had, but I knew the business at the junction needed to get finished.

I stuffed my sunglasses into the pocket of my duster, glad that the glare of the day had finally passed.

Hiding had always been part of my work in the army. I had never liked it. That's where my mind turned as I crouched in the ruins of a small building a hundred meters from the junction tower. Hiding in a hole just isn't where a proud lawman ought to be, yet I'd been there an hour waiting for Ben to come back with Court.

My legs creaked as I stood, reminding me of the bruises I'd gotten earlier in the day. My whole left leg just about seized up from stiffness, and my head throbbed like I'd been pistol whipped.

Sam's skidder was hidden there too. I pulled the cover off of it and kicked away the dried grass I had used to conceal it. Sitting on it felt good, like I belonged in the open sky. There was a reason people rode those things. The sense of freedom was intoxicating.

I kicked the engine on and winced as its boom echoed across the open expanse. So much for hiding. I made sure my hat was secure on my head, and I launched into the air, heading straight for the tower. It was time to revert back to the original plan.

The tower was flat on top and forty meters across on each side. The far side held a row of skidders that were similar to Sam's, each with its own modifications and eccentricities. Groups of kids were scattered around the roof, engaged in whatever kids do when they're where they shouldn't be.

Figuring surprise was my best advantage, I came in hard. I cranked the jets on the skidder, swooped in low, below the edge of the tower. At the last second, I crested the tower and jumped, rolling as I hit the roof.

The nearest punks didn't see it coming. I ran to the first and grabbed him.

I felt a tug at the tails of my coat and another at my arm. The twang of electric gunfire echoed through the dusk, and I struggled to find its source.

Then I had the kid. Three fingers from my metal hand locked onto him. Two fingers gripped his neck while the other wrapped all the way over the back of his head to grip an eye socket. He was mine. I thrust him in front of me.

"Nobody move!" I shouted.

Just then Sam's skidder hit the roof and crashed into the row of bikes parked along the far edge. Two of them fell off, crashing to the ground below. A particularly shiny one teetered on the edge. I wasn't there to make friends.

The roof exploded in a flurry of activity. The guy I was holding started crying, wailing for help. He was a kid to me, but if I had to guess, I'd have said he was probably twenty. The kids who were close enough to cause me trouble started to circle around. One of them caught a bullet for his efforts, but not from me. Whoever was shooting didn't seem to care much. The kid backed off.

I spun my rag doll around so that he was between the shooter and me. Another shot whizzed past my ear.

"I just want to talk to Court, kids," I said. "Not here for trouble."

"Fuck that!" Some kid far enough away to be out of danger saw no trouble in egging the rest of us on.

The third skidder—the shiny one—shifted a little, piercing the dusk with the sound of scraping metal.

It was getting darker. These modders probably all had night vision, so they were going to have an advantage. A person could say they already had it.

Another shot flew past, but this time I spotted the shooter.

I drew my gun, flipped off the safety, stared the guy in the eyes, and aimed. I recognized the kid. His chrome teeth sparkled in what was left of the sunset. It was the runner who had escaped earlier that day. The guy with the legs.

"Put the gun down, Legs. I do not care if you are trespassing or engaging in illegal activity here." Again, I was lying, but they didn't need to know that. "This here is about a murder that I intend to solve. I just need some cooperation, and I need to talk to someone named Court."

There was hesitation in his eyes. That cocky chrome smile was starting to fade. I waited for understanding to flicker through his eyes before I continued.

"Do you understand what's happening here, son?" I dropped the guy I was holding. I no longer needed a shield.

Legs lowered his weapon.

"Court. Now."

He seemed to be considering something. Maybe the metal half of his brain was weighing the risks of various actions. He could weigh all he wanted. He didn't have a chance.

There was a flicker of understanding in the kid's shiny little eyes.

I wasn't aiming at him.

The best looking bike on the whole roof was in my sights. One shot and it would be over the edge.

I heard something heavy fall deep inside the tower. The floor in the center of the roof started to open. A square several meters wide opened and a rusty cage elevator screeched upward. In it were two people. The first was a woman. She was tall and unbelievably skinny. Her extra pair of arms was so realistic that I had trouble telling which were her real ones. She had long, flowing red hair and eyes that glowed like fireflies on a warm summer night. She wore a cloak of shimmering metal that seemed to move against the wind.

The other person in the elevator was Ben. His spiky hair was somewhat in disarray, but he seemed otherwise unharmed. He looked at me with a mixture of fear and hatred.

"Please, Mr. Crow, lower your weapon." Her voice was unnatural and ethereal. It flowed with the heavy air and carried with it an accent I had never heard before.

I didn't lower my weapon.

"You may not understand. That is my ride. It is very special."

I did understand. I did not lower my weapon.

"I am told you are a reasonable man. You see, that vehicle is powered with a solid fusion reactor coil. It's quite powerful, but a bullet from such a crude weapon as yours would likely pierce its containment and kill us all."

I hesitated but still didn't lower my weapon. I looked from her to the bike and back again, cursing myself for failing to hide my hesitation.

She took a few steps forward, pulling Ben out of the elevator. "You think you are threatening my skidder, but you are really threatening us all." She smiled a wicked sort of hyena smile. "I assure you, we will not kill you or your little friend."

I holstered my weapon.

"Thank you."

With a fluid motion, she swept up Ben and threw him in my direction. He hit the roof hard and skidded to a stop.

"Now be gone."

"One question."

She raised an eyebrow. "It will cost."

"I bet." I reached down to help Ben up. He shot a look of hatred at me and brushed aside my hand.

"I had it under control," he whispered through gritted teeth.

"Tell me, Courtney," I started.

"Court is fine."

"Miss Court, I am here on the trail of a murderer. I believe your boys had dealings with the victim last night. Some of them might've roughed him up a little."

"None of these are questions."

"No, ma'am. They are not. My question is, who followed Mr. Brown back to his house."

Court smiled, revealing a row of shiny sharp teeth. She took a graceful step forward, closing the distance between us unbelievably fast. She was nearly a head taller than me. Her perfect lips brushed my ear and she whispered her answer.

"Both of them?" I asked in reply.

She pulled back just a little and gazed into my eyes and gave an almost imperceptible nod. Her green irises danced with mischief. With one slender hand, she cupped my jawline gently and turned my head from side to side.

"Handsome, in a way," she said. "Charmingly soft."

With a downward snap, she raked three fingers across my jaw. Her keenly sharpened claws shredded lines into my cheek from just below my eye all the way down to my chin. I did not flinch.

Blood ran down my face.

"We have all we need, Ben. Let's go." I looked Court in the eyes, noting the amused look she was giving me.

Ben didn't move.

"Ben," I said. "It's time to go." I didn't take my eyes off of Court, but I could hear a murmur of amusement moving through the crowd.

I set my jaw, feeling the sting of the wound on my cheek. Pain was creeping back now. My adrenaline was dropping fast. My head throbbed and it wasn't helping my mood. With my right hand, I brushed back my coat, revealing the pistol holstered there.

The murmur of amusement exploded into a cacophony of laughter. One high-pitched wail pierced the rest. It was that runner who had mocked me earlier in the day outside of the Dry Goat. His mouth opened wide in laughter, metal teeth showing in the eerie dusk.

"Tell me something, man of the law," said Court. "Did you kill Sammer the Hammer for his skidder, or did you just happen to steal it off of his corpse."

I was taken aback. "Sam was dead when we found him."

"Was he?"

"The bike's not stolen. It's confiscated."

"Interesting how a choice of words can change things." She took a step back. "Confiscating a bike sounds so much more legitimate, does it not?"

I turned my back on Court and her followers. Struggling to mask my limp, I strode confidently over to the skidder. With my metal hand I grabbed the handlebars and pulled the vehicle around to face the crowd. I was conflicted but determined to not let it show. How could I leave the kid behind when just hours ago all I had wanted was to protect him. This gang of criminals was no protection for an eleven-year-old boy, yet I couldn't think of any way to get him out of there safely.

I found the dial that controlled the jets and dialed it all the way up.

"Boy," I said. "You got one last chance to man up. Come chase down your father's killer. Make it right."

The boy spoke. "Ain't nothin' right about what you do, lawman." He pulled what looked like a small, black pistol from the back of his pants and pointed it at me. "You fucked this up all day, old man. Thanks for the ride but you'd best be going now."

What I did next was stupid.

In my defense, I couldn't exactly leave the biker gang without dispensing some form of justice. I was in the justice business, after all. They were criminals. They terrorized the good people of my town and someone had to do something about it. Also, any biker stupid enough to park right on the unprotected edge of a three-story building ought to be taught a lesson. I knew that what I did wouldn't break up the gang, but I thought it might at least slow them down.

It didn't help that I was made a little dumb by rage and pain. Some of the finer points in my plan may have been miscalculated or misinformed.

I tipped my hat to Court.

My metal hand clamped hard onto the middle of the handlebars, and I punched the ignition with my human hand.

Explosive blue flames went off like a gunshot. The skidder launched into the darkening night and the hot air blasted my face. Behind me, skidders slid off the edge of the building. Court's ride teetered on the edge.

Howls of amusement transformed into cries of rage. I dropped hard, banked left. Gunshots went off, but nothing came close—not yet.

"Shoot the bastard down!" Ben shouted and wasted his clip in my direction. He might as well have been firing at the night sky for all the good it did. Others were shooting now too. Something pinged off of the rear fender.

I swooped down below the edge of the building and then pulled up hard above. I was close now, so I kept my movements erratic.

Below, Court slowly drew a long, slender tube that was half a meter long and shined like a chrome spear.

With my head low, I gunned the ignition hard. One pass was all I was likely to get.

I rammed Court's bike as I passed far too close to the crowd. Another shot rang off of Sam's skidder.

Court's bike fell. I dropped hard to get below the side of the building in order to make myself a harder target. They'd have to run to the edge to get a good shot at me.

It was a bad idea.

Court had not been bluffing when she'd said the bike was explosive.

I felt a tug on my chest. It didn't hurt. It felt like someone had tweaked it just a little. I glanced down to see blood welling up through the coat from just below the left nipple. The console on my bike shot sparks from a new hole.

I glanced back and saw Court's gleaming eyes staring me down. She was pointing her thin chrome tube in my direction.

That's when the explosion hit.

Being hit by a concussive blast hurts a lot less than a person might expect. One second I was looking back at the tower, waiting for the next shot to finish me off. Then there was a light from below, the flare lit up the night like it was the middle of the day.

Then there was nothing.

Chapter 13

Being hit by a concussive blast hurts a lot more than a person might expect.

"Eep, eep."

For a full minute, I lay there with my eyes closed, trying to figure out what she was saying.

"Eep, eep."

She just kept repeating it. My head hurt, but that fit pretty good with what the rest of my body was up to.

"Eep, eep."

Wind whipped past, tugging my coat, my face, my hair. I briefly wondered where my hat had gone, as if that was the most pressing issue at the moment.

It wasn't.

"Eep, eep."

I couldn't figure out what she was saying. It didn't even sound like words to me, and I'd be damned if I was going to decipher what she was trying to say if she wasn't even using words. Slowly, I forced one eye open.

That's when it all came back: the explosion, the narrow tube that Court had been pointing at me, and my hurried escape from the angry biker gang. How long had I been out?

It was dark. I could feel the wind jerking the bike around as it sped through the air. My metallic hand still gripped the middle of the handlebars, which explained why

I hadn't fallen off. The bike was moving fast—not at full throttle, but close.

"Eep, eep."

It wasn't a girl's voice. It was a warning. A light on the dash blinked in rhythm with the noise, probably indicating a lack of fucl.

My metal grip left kinks in the handlebars when I let go. A swift manipulation of the controls slowed me down and carried me to the ground. I powered down the jets and switched everything off before slumping off the bike and landing on my back.

There were no stars—only a boiling mass of fast-moving clouds. Yellow lightning lit up the sky from time to time, but no rain fell. The megastorm was coming. It wouldn't be there that night, by the look of it, but it was on its way. You could always see those things coming for a few days, which always made me wonder how people ever got caught out in them.

It looked as though I might soon enough find out.

My bike was low on fuel. If I had been unconscious long enough to run out of fuel at nearly full speed, I could be hundreds of kilometers away—maybe a thousand. I wondered if I had been moving in a straight line. Regardless, I certainly wasn't going to walk back, and there probably wasn't enough fuel to ride back. Also, without the stars it was going to be difficult to tell which direction I'd gone.

I sat up.

Something never sat well with me whenever I had to depend on technology. I never trusted it. The skills I learned from my father had never let me down: shooting, tracking, hunting. My mother's dislike for tech kept me natural, even in an era when raising a kid without enhanced eyes or skin was considered borderline abusive. She taught me how to see the world and make my own observations, even when discovery via tech would have been so much easier. Even when I was a kid I understood the value of finding water in the desert. Tracking animals or men didn't come easy, but I always knew it was a skill that wouldn't let me down. I had used it since then too. It was always hard, but it always worked.

Tech comes easy, makes life easy. Then it breaks. When that happened, if you were tech, you were broken too.

Lately, though, I'd been more dependent on technology. The strength of my arm could win my fights. The scans from my glow cube or sunglasses gave me easy information. That skidder got me where I needed to be faster than anything I had ever ridden. Only, now it didn't.

I had to admit it; I was addicted to tech, and there was no way out. I fumbled in my pocket for the sunglasses. Those sunglasses could let me communicate with Trish. She could have gotten out there to pick me up. I couldn't think of any other option.

The glasses had exploded all over the inside of my pocket. This confused me at first. Then I poked a finger through the chest pocket of my duster. The hole went all the way through. In fact, it went down to my chest where I spotted a small hole in my skin that looked like it had already sealed itself. My back and the back of my duster had similar holes. What the hell kind of bullet passes through its victim without causing any damage?

I remembered the sparks from the console. Using my enormously strong metal fingers, I pried back a piece of the broken steel so that I could see the skidder's internal damage. It didn't take long for me to discover two things. First, I did not in any way understand the internal workings of the modern flying vehicle.

Second, the bullet that had damaged the console and likely passed through me was nothing more than a single sliver of black metal.

I flopped back to the ground and stared up at the boiling sky.

Maybe there was justice in the world. There I was, dying in the desert just like the kid whose bike I'd stolen. Court was right. Whether you called it confiscating or stealing, it was the same damn thing. How many people had died back at the junction? Had the explosion been enough to topple the building? Thinking back, I didn't think so, but that didn't make me feel any less guilty.

I had tried to save Ben when he didn't even want to be saved. Then I'd put his life at risk because of my own anger.

Was it my anger? The question came in to my head in a flash, and I didn't know what to think. Of course it was my anger. Whose else would it be?

There was something strange. It was strange that I wasn't numb. I had spent so many years in suffocating numbness that I had forgotten what real passion felt like. Real anger at injustice drove a man to do great things. Since the war, since I had been forever mutilated, the passion had been gone. Justice was a habit—something I fought for because I didn't know what else to do.

I fought for it but what did it mean to me anymore?

That whole day I had been having odd mood swings. Could it have been something connected with the case? Was it something to do with Ma Brown or Trish or maybe the man in black who kept trying to track me down? Whatever it was had triggered strong emotions in me. In contrast, my last twenty years looked like a gray waste.

I thought of how nice it might be if the man in black had found me right about then. Maybe I would have been able to clear up some questions and get a ride back to town. I wasn't counting on such luck, though. If I wanted to find a way out of this, I'd need to do it myself.

Still, I didn't move.

The question still lingered in my mind. *Should* I find a way out? If this was the world dispensing justice, then maybe just staying still was the easiest way to go. My whole body hurt. My head pulsed with an ache like none I'd ever known. My chest stung where I'd been shot, as did my back, just below the shoulder blade. I felt like I had been bruised from head to toe. I could sleep like this. It would be one final night in the great feral frontier. One more night under the rolling sky.

My eyes drifted shut.

Ma Brown used emo chips to handle her herd. She transmitted her own feelings to them to better control otherwise unmanageable creatures. It made sense. I'd felt rage at that milk distribution man from this morning. It seemed like that was weeks ago. I had cried at the thought of Mrs. Brown being alone mourning her husband's death. I shuddered at the memory of the dream I'd had in Trish's cruiser. Were any of these emotions my own? I'd felt a surge of protectiveness when the topic at the dinner table had been Ben's safety. Her feelings were being pushed onto me, and I very much would have liked to know how this was happening. More importantly, I would have liked to know why.

That, however, wasn't enough to get me off of the ground. I forced my eyes open.

It must have been the milk. The same nannies that controlled the herd and contaminated the milk supply were running around in my system and mucking with my emotions. I'd had two doses, once in the morning and again for lunch. Had any of my emotions been real that day?

Something passed overhead. For a moment, I thought the man in black might actually have tracked me down. It wasn't him, though. Silhouetted by the flashes in the sky, the black shape swooped around three times and then landed on the skidder. It was a bird.

It was a crow.

The crow stared at me with its pale yellow eyes. It clacked its beak and stretched its black wings.

An omen. My mother always described crows as omens, but my muddled brain was having trouble sorting it out. The crow peered at me with those oddly intelligent eyes.

I slowly turned my head toward it to get a better look. "What the hell do you want, bird?"

It folded its wings and shifted restlessly from one foot to the other.

"Come a little early for the feast, huh?" With protesting muscles, I sat up.

For the first time since I had landed, I took in my surroundings. The crow and I were on a hillside. Scraggly grasses covered the dry earth and danced feverishly to summon the coming storm. I tasted fine Texas soil in my mouth, a sandy mixture whipped up by the wind. Fifty meters down the rocky slope ran a small stream. Fifty meters up the hill, an overhang of jagged sandstone blocked the wind and spun it into a frenzy.

The crow spread its wings and flapped but didn't take off. It watched me with eyes that seemed to know what I was thinking.

Lightning flashed through the clouds again. It had yet to arc to the ground, but those flashes were enough to light up the world. Beyond the crow, I spotted a slight glimmer of hope: a stout, black building, nearly invisible in the night.

My knees cracked as I forced them to bend. Muscles screamed at me and dizziness threatened to land me back on my ass. Still, I forced myself to stand.

The crow took flight.

My heart raced. My jaw hardened. I felt a swell of contempt at all of the old people and their omens. My mother had taught me something of the Hopi tradition, but what did she know? One eighth Hopi does not make a person an expert. She was removed enough from the old ways that there was no way to know what came from that proud tradition and what had been invented in subsequent years. So much had been lost to casinos and cultural warfare. When the language was lost, so was memory. The Hopi tradition was dead long before I ever heard of it. It had always fascinated me, though. What little my mother had shared rang true and drove me. Whatever life was like back then, it must have been better than what we had to suffer through.

The people who were my ancestors, the peacemakers, they were all dead. There was nothing left of them, so why should I cling to their ways just to end up dead in the desert? If the crow was their omen of death and if justice dictated that my time was up, then I was through with both.

I took a step.

My ma had talked about the old ways when I was little. She had talked it up when I was a kid, but she'd only really taken the parts she'd liked. She'd told stories of the old religion, but they'd been just that: stories.

I took another step, then another. I brushed past the bike and moved steadily downhill. Ahead I saw a stream at the bottom of the hill; the gentle sound of moving water reached my ears. The sky boiled. Lightning was my only light.

I'd always worshipped the old ways as I'd wanted them to be. A land with civilization in retreat looks like a land with civilization on the frontier. The analogy had always fit. Law was a commodity. Order was at a premium. I always had felt it was my duty to be the peacemaker, even when I went off to war to fight for my people. Even when we lost.

The stream was warm, warmer than the night air. I splashed some water on my face and felt its fingers running down my chest. I breathed a deep breath and felt the water's life-giving energy seeping into my body. I drank deep and stood to walk more confidently.

How can a man follow a tradition he hardly knows? The same way a man follows a tradition that he knows well: blindly.

Movement from above caught my eye. It was the crow again, gliding silently through the air. It seemed to hover in place above me, gliding against the wind and keeping my slow pace.

If the crow was an omen of my death and I survived, then the meaning was clear. It was time to set aside the tradition of my ancestors. It was time to set aside justice. What was justice, anyway? Was it the same as revenge, the way confiscating was the same as stealing? It seemed to me on that dark night that there might not be any difference at all.

My mother had left when I was young. I didn't know why. I probably never would. I suspect it had something to do with my brother Conrad's death or my father's reaction to it. After that day, I had noticed a hardening in my father's eyes. He had been left to raise me, but his ideas of tradition and peacekeeping were much harsher. He was a lawman back then. When he couldn't take that anymore, he became a bounty hunter. My love of tradition still existed, but it was his idea of tradition that I followed, not my ma's.

By the time I arrived at the black building, my pains had left me. My heart still raced but my muscles now ached only for action. Without breaking stride, I went straight up to the door and kicked it open.

Inside, lights flickered to life. I stepped in and breathed years of stale air and dust. It was exactly what I'd thought it was: an outpost.

During the Texan Civil War, there had been a number of these outposts. They had been designed using low-tech so that they wouldn't be noticed by an increasingly high-tech enemy. They used low-wattage lights, analog two-way radios and repeaters, and all manner of low-tech projectile weaponry.

The weapons were gone, of course. The place had probably been looted twenty years ago, just after the war. The squat, desk-sized radio was still there. Every one of these stations I'd run across in my years as a sheriff had a working radio and working lights. People only tend to loot items of value, and these things were constructed in such a way as to be nearly worthless—sturdy, but worthless.

Hardly anyone used analog signals. There was only one man I knew who did. He used it all the time when he needed to stay off the networks. He used it when he was hunting people.

I grabbed the radio and pressed the transmit button.

"Come in, Big Blackbird." I paused. "Come in, Big Blackbird. This is Little Blackbird. Big Blackbird, you out there?"

The crow, the real one, landed just outside the door and looked at me. It tilted its head to one side as if questioning me.

"Not you," I said.

It stretched its wings.

"On your way, then," I said to the crow. "Thanks for the wakeup, but I got no need for omens today."

The crow flew away just as the radio crackled to life.

"Little Blackbird, this is Big Blackbird."

I smiled, a little surprised that he'd caught the signal so quickly. "Big Blackbird, I'm in a bit of a bind here. Mind picking up some fuel and helping a guy out?"

There was a pause. "Be a pleasure, son."

"'Preciate it.'"

Chapter 14

I sat across from Pa and chewed through the gristly steak like I hadn't eaten in a week, even though the feast at the ranch had only been twelve hours previous.

The dim light of the old diner did nothing to conceal its griminess. Shadows melted with stains in the corners of *every* wall. It was hard to tell when one started and the other ended. There were decorations on the walls, dimly lit flickering neon advertisements for beers that hadn't been brewed in a hundred years. This place was a throwback, some sort of retro trend that used to be fashionable thirty years ago. Pa, the owner, and I were the only people around.

When I finished the steak, I set down my knife and used an old rag to wipe the juices out of my stubble. The wind howled outside. I squinted at the window to see if I could spot the skidder. After we had reloaded the solid fuel repository, it had run well enough to get me here, but there was something wrong with the controls. I reached into my pocket and fingered the black metal needle I had pulled from the machine.

"Storm's comin'," said Pa after one particularly strong gust rattled the windows. He was still chewing at his own steak, carefully pulling out gristle and fat and setting it aside.

I nodded. "Yup."

"You into some sort of trouble out there?"

Pa liked to cut right to the heart of things. He sat there across from me wearing a gambler-style wide-brimmed hat, pristine like he'd just bought it. I knew he hadn't. He just took good care of his stuff. His suit was in similar condition, with a gray nanofiber mesh for the coat and something that looked like violet silk for his shirt. His tie was the traditional Texas string tie, cinched tight so that the loose wrinkles of his neck bulged up over the collar. The impeccable lines of his expensive suit contrasted with the sagging form of his aged body. Gloved hands moved with a strength and confidence unexpected for such an old codger. Hunting had been a lucrative profession for the old man, and he was able to afford the best in tech—and he wasn't afraid to show it off.

I wondered what trouble he thought I was in. If I were in trouble, I didn't think it would be something I'd want to talk with him about. In fact, I had only stayed to share a meal with him because he had offered to pay and I was famished.

"There's trouble, Pa, but not for me."

The old man's chewing slowed and he raised an eyebrow. A few heavy minutes of silence passed.

"Ma ever tell you about the Hopi?" I finally asked.

He smiled at me. "No more a them around, son."

"Sure, sure. But did she talk about it?"

Another minute of silence passed. He put down his fork and looked me right in the eyes. "She did. She used to talk about it. Talked about it to you too. I get the feeling you listened 'bout as much as I did." He chuckled to himself as if it was a joke.

"Well." I ran my fingers through my hair, wishing I still had my hat. "I sure wish I had listened, is all. There was a crow out there when I was stuck. Think it might've been a death omen or something."

He nodded.

"You know anything about that, Pa?"

"Nope." A screen of shapes, letters, and lights flashed in front of the old man's face, originating, I guessed, from his immaculate hat. "You want me to look it up?"

I waved my hand in front of his face, dispersing the floating images. "No, Pa. I don't really."

He ground his teeth and his voice took on an agitated tone. "Son, you gotta stop fearing the tech. You always had a damn problem with it. Ain't done you no harm."

"Ain't done me no good, neither."

The old man glanced over his shoulder at the owner of the diner, a dark-skinned guy with a fat gut soaked with grease and a silver eye that flashed with light from time to time.

"Look," Pa said in a low voice. "You in some sort of trouble? I can help you out, you know."

"Pa, look," I felt like a delinquent kid again. "I'm not in any trouble. I should be asking you if you're in trouble, but I don't think either of us wants to know the answer." We both knew he had a habit of skirting the edges of the law.

He grinned at that, showing me his yellow teeth. "Suit yourself."

We passed the time in silence for a while. When Pa had finished his steak, the owner brought over two slices of absolutely dreadful lemon meringue pie. The meringue was charred on the top and soggy on the bottom. The lemon was bitter. It was the best I'd had in years.

Pa broke the silence. "Genevieve was a lovely woman. Better than I ever deserved." His voice had taken on a wistful tone. "She loved nature. Loved being outside, even after nature decided to crap right out on us."

He took a bite of pie and held it in his mouth as if savoring its awful flavor.

"Thing is, I think she really might have followed some of the old traditions." He looked up at me. "I don't think she really believed in omens and shit, though."

"Didn't think so."

"Don't you go all soft on me, son. There's no reason to worry. Ain't nothin' out there you can't handle."

I had never heard my father talk like that. I always got the idea that he believed in me, but he had never really said it. It worried me.

"Pa," I said. "You remember when Conrad died? What happened?"

The old man's expression got dark. There was a flash of hatred, then one of sadness and resignation. "They said we was poachers. Said we were stealing from the government by living off of the land."

There was another long pause as he took a slow bite of pie and chewed it very deliberately.

"The gang that got him, they were nothin' but a bunch of punks. Kids doin' someone else's dirty work. Jackals. I don't know. They killed your brother. Shot him in the middle of the night and didn't have the decency to come and shoot me too. They figured I'd learn my lesson."

"Lesson?" I was amazed that he'd said so much. Conrad's death had always been a forbidden topic.

"You kill something of ours, we'll kill something of yours." The old man raised a forkful of pie to his mouth, then thought better of it and set it down. "There's a goddamn lesson for you. It was pretty soon after that I started hunting people."

"You kill those punks?"

He narrowed one eye at me. "This my son talking or the lawman?"

I scowled at him.

"Yeah, I killed them. You were there too but probably too young to remember it. Wasn't nothin' to me at the time. I didn't feel a damn bit of guilt."

I nodded. I figured he was lying, but I knew better than to call him on it.

"They say killin' and revenge don't help anything, son. They say it doesn't make you feel better and it doesn't solve any problems." The old man took off his hat and leaned forward, looking me straight in the eyes. "They're wrong."

"It's not justice, though. It's not order or law."

"Nope."

"It's just hard, you know?"

"You lookin' to do the same thing?"

"Nope," I said too fast.

"Well, you watch out when you do. There's all kinds a trouble out there, and some of it you don't want to be messing with."

I nodded.

"Son, you and me are Crows. You know what a Crow does when there's a storm coming?"

I made no response. I had heard the lecture a dozen times before.

"Crows leave when there's a storm comin'. They get out of there and find a safe place to ride it out. They don't fly into it, J.D. That's how they survive."

I remembered the first time he had told me that years ago. I'd been getting ready to fight in the Civil War. I hadn't listened back then. Sitting there in front of my pa, I thought about how different my life might have been if I had.

"There's trouble coming, son." He shook his head. "Trouble like you ain't seen before. Even in your little war."

"You've been sayin' that for twenty years."

"It's been true for twenty years. You just gotta open your eyes."

I looked around the grimy diner. The light flickered sickly in its socket as the owner polished a filthy counter with a filthy rag. "My eyes are open, Pa. I'm not seeing it."

A forkful of pie found itself stuck between the plate and Pa's mouth. He kept raising it halfway and then putting it down again. Finally, he set the fork down.

"What's anyone done that you got trouble with, boy?"

I thought for a minute. Daniel Brown had been murdered. I hardly knew him, though. Sam's death had been on my watch. While that got me riled up, it didn't really warrant the sort of anger I was feeling. What was it?

"They fucked with my people, Pa." I instinctively looked around for a hat that wasn't there. "They made us weak. They made us suck the land dry so we could feed them. They told us we'd fought them to a draw twenty years ago. Then they proceeded to take from us everything that was ever valuable. And for it, they gave us nothing. Well, there's nothing left for us. There's no law and order anymore. There's not one damn shred of justice left in this land that isn't made by me, personally, and I'm tired of it."

I stood and ran my fingers through my hair again. The old man just smiled up at me.

"I'm done with it. I always thought tradition was the foundation everything else was built on. Even the outlaws and modders didn't mean anything unless they had something to rebel against. I thought the old beliefs were something to be respected. Laws meant something, you know? There was something that said what's right and what's wrong."

"God's been dead a long time, son."

"It ain't some god I'm talking about. There was that crow out in the desert. Now I know the crow's an omen. Lot of that stuff's been forgotten, but I know the crow's an omen. Well, when I saw that bird I knew it was my time. It must have been, right? Except when it came my time I thought I'd always just take it. I didn't. That crow of death came for me and I turned my back on it."

His grin was something comical now. He looked like a proud father ready to pat his little boy on the head. Then his expression soured.

"Son," he said. "You're going to want to know something. I got a call for a bounty just before I heard you on the horn."

I turned to leave. "I'm not going to be a hunter like you, Pa. Even if I'm giving up being a lawman."

I nodded to the owner as I left the diner and pushed my way out into the heavy night air. Fat raindrops were just starting to fall, making big dark marks on the dusty parking lot. Pa stood up to follow me, but I didn't slow. In a few strides I got to my bike and swung a leg over it. The engine roared to life.

"Son, wait! You gotta see this." He pulled out a glow cube showing a wall of flickering text. "Got it just about an hour ago." He was shouting over the roar of the jets. "Wanted for the murder of Daniel Brown! Bounty's out, dead or alive!"

"Who?"

He swiped across the screen a few times and then turned it to show me the photo. It was the same stock photo of me that the station used to use for promotional items.

"Who the hell do you think?"

Our eyes met. For the first time, I thought I saw concern in his expression. There was something resembling what you'd expect from a worried father.

"Who signed it?" I shouted over the roar of the jets. Fat, hot raindrops were rolling off of the old man's hat and pouring to the ground. They felt good on my face and washed the grime out of my hair.

"There's a new sheriff in Dead Oak." Pa read from the cube's text. "Sheriff Balon Swayle. Watch your back, son."

I punched the accelerator. The skidder bucked a few times, pulling to one side and then the other, showing a will it'd never shown before it'd been shot. I wrestled it under control, yanked the bars up, and rocketed into the air.

Chapter 15

The night had been almost over when I'd left the diner. I really had intended to skip town. Justice would sort itself out without me. Or it wouldn't. I'd feel guilty about leaving, but sometimes a person just needs to carry around a little guilt. When Pa showed me the bounty on my head, though, I knew I couldn't just run. Bounty hunters had a knack for efficiency and brutality. I needed to figure out what was going on and resolve it before heading out of town. Even if I managed to cross into Canada, I could never really be sure I was free.

According to Court there were two people around the night Daniel Brown died. One of them was a beautiful lady with braided hair and tanned skin. The other one was the preacher Henry Sharpe.

That's why I was there stuffed like a sardine into Henry Sharpe's church. I'd ridden through the red sunrise and arrived just as the congregation was finishing stuffing itself into the dark red hogan twenty kilometers outside of Dead Oak. The building resembled a bunker more than a church, but the cross outside marked it as a place of worship.

Old Jack was there, along with the dentist Frederick Cornsley. I recognized a dozen faces in the crowd. Religion had been nearly dead and marginalized for generations, so seeing so many people I knew in such a small place was a little disconcerting. I had no idea who might have arrived before me to hide in the crowd. I kept my head down.

Baptists, the southern variety in particular, are the most rotten stink ever made on this dying planet. They preached harder than I'd ever seen any fanatic preach. They had been a thorn in my side for years, figuring their god's law was a few steps above mine. They might have been right, but I still had to work hard to keep them in line.

Worship and religious ritual had for the most part been eliminated from the common vernacular for several generations. Mostly, talk of Jesus was limited to cussing and fairy tales. Those who still considered themselves faithful were still around, but for the most part faith was put in things like technology and guns.

There were still a few Christians around. Once, years ago, a group of Southern Baptists started kidnapping folks. It wasn't obvious at first, but I picked up on it. The thing was, the folks they kidnapped never pressed for justice. They'd always convert. Then they'd forgive.

Nothing annoys a man of justice quite like forgiveness.

A little muscle needed to be applied to the Baptists so they'd stop doing it. Southern Baptists. Nobody even knows what they're south of, but they insist on the name. It's tradition, I suppose. It was a callback to a time when Southern Baptists were a respected organization. I respected that. Word was they had been around since before Texas was a country.

All of this contributed to my discomfort as I sat in the back of the church. The place was concrete and packed with nearly a hundred congregants. It smelled of sweat and kerosene and tobacco smoke.

In the front of the church, on a small stage flanked by two man-sized fake ficus plants, Henry Sharpe started to preach. He had the same square-jawed profile and plastic hair of the younger, sleazier Billy Sharpe. I guessed the two were father and son, but how they were involved with the

Brown murder I could not guess. Maybe I could have put it together, but my mind was occupied with more pressing concerns.

There was a new sheriff in town, but normally sheriffs were selected by election. On rare occasions a judge can assign a temporary replacement, but that sort of thing only happens when a sheriff goes rogue or dies. Since the town didn't have a sitting judge, the appointment would come from the city. What reason could there be for bureaucrats in the city to send someone new, and who was he?

Balon Swayle, that's who he was. Pa had given me the name and I'd heard some folks talking about him in murmurs at the back of the church. He wasn't well liked. In fact, he'd already gained a reputation for cruelty when he rounded up most of the Cinco Armas and tossed them in jail. Not that anyone thought tossing that lot in jail was such a bad thing. Everyone he locked up got all of their tech crippled, sometimes in a permanent fashion. This man was not out to make friends.

Suddenly, I found myself paying attention to the sermon.

"They shall be cleansed of their sin!" With his arms raised, the preacher was giving it his all. "Washed of their murders. Forgiven their adultery! They will give back all that they stole!"

The white-haired preacher paced from side to side on an open stage like a tiger stalking its prey. Each sin was spat out with greater emphasis.

"They will hold no other god but God!"

"Hallelujah!" A woman in the front was so overcome with feelings she fell to the floor in front of the altar. I furrowed my brow. I recognized her from somewhere, but I was having trouble placing it.

The congregation was wild in general and I felt it. My heart raced and I was having trouble focusing my thoughts. I stood with everyone else and turned my eyes upward.

"Praise be to the lord!" The preacher said.

"Praise be to the lord!" The congregation said as one.

"There is one mightier, my friends." His voice became soft and we all leaned in to hear better. My heart still raced and sweat formed on my brow. "I have come. I have come into your midst and I shall not baptize you in water."

A tense murmur rippled through the congregation.

"I will not cleanse your sins with the mud that the city man leaves for us."

The congregation dropped into silence. I felt it. I was hanging on every word. My emotions raging in whatever direction he pulled. It felt like electricity was pulsing through the air. I was inspired, elated. That's when I knew what the motive for everything was. This was not *my* passion. This was the activity of a million nanomachines manipulating my emotions.

This was Ma Brown's passion, but knowing its source didn't seem to help me control it.

"I!" Sharpe gave a decidedly un-Christian emphasis to the word. "Will baptize you in flames!"

He raised his hands straight to the sky and flames shot up from the floor. My elation turned briefly to panic, but the flames weren't hot—not too hot, anyway. They still scalded where they touched bare skin, but nothing was set ablaze.

I admit that I may have let out a holler. It was a cry of joy at a rebirth in which I then had complete faith. Faith was a most intricate and intense byproduct of the emotions that had so powerfully swept over me. It had taken me in entirely. I basked in those cleansing flames, soaking in their promise of a pure soul. I felt as if the sins were seared from my fouled soul.

A babbling was flowing from my mouth, and soon I became aware of its contents. I was giving an account of my sins. I spoke of the skidder I had stolen and of Sam, who had died from my neglect. I spoke of all the men I had sent to the Canadian border to work in the Des Moines flood plains. I spoke of the men I had killed—those who I knew were guilty and those who might not have been. Thou shalt not kill, the lord had said, and I had killed.

Something broke me from my spell. It wasn't greater or more profound. I'd have been more proud if it were. It was, however, something I thought I would never see again in my life. Sometimes a person can miss something so badly that it pulls him away from god. In this case, I suspect it was that material thing that saved me from the power of that Baptist preacher.

Through the flaming, writhing crowd I saw the one thing that had any chance of pulling me from my newfound faith.

I saw my hat.

A person could probably have come up with a dozen theories on what my hat was doing there. My hat had fallen off sometime around the tower explosion at the Junction. A fully functioning brain might have come up with some explanation for how my hat had ended up in this church. My brain was not fully functioning. I was still in the thrall of faith. My brain sought meaning without reason.

Yet, some part of me protested. I saw the hat so briefly—that brown Stetson with the black cord and the nick where a bullet once nearly took off my head. Nobody was wearing it, but someone was holding it. That person raised it briefly. I just caught a glimpse of it through the rolling orange flames.

I needed to know who had my hat.

My new love for God had to wait. I swallowed those feelings down and set them aside. I'd gotten disturbingly good at this during my many years as sheriff.

The tide of flames was ebbing now. The last flickers played across the sinners all around me. I shouldered my way through the reverent crowd, ignoring their pleas for forgiveness and trying very hard to ignore the confessions of their sins out of respect for their privacy.

The middle aisle was packed, but I managed to muscle my way forward. Once, when I risked a glance upward, I saw the good Reverend Sharpe looking my way. It would not have been good to be recognized there, so I slowed my progress and tried harder to blend in.

"Benjamin Brown," I said in a low voice when I saw the kid not two meters away gripping my hat in two hands. His mother was there too, along with the rest of the Brown clan.

Everybody was in the throes of a passion like I had never seen, but none quite so much as Ma Brown. She had thrown herself to the ground and wept great big tears all over the floor. I do believe she was actually gnashing her teeth. I backed into the crowd, eager not to be noticed. As I did so, I caught Ma Brown's mournful voice calling out louder than all the rest.

She said, "I killed him. Lord, forgive me. I killed my Danny. Lord, forgive me!"

A church can be such an enlightening place.

The place had an emergency door near the pulpit, but the main door was near the back. My senses seemed to be returning to me, even though I could feel my heart pounding like it was trying to escape. My vision was starting to focus, and the feeling of unwarranted elation was starting to fade. The only reasonable chance for escape was the back door. I moved carefully back into a position in the rear of the sanctuary, keeping my head low and my hair draped down to cover my face.

The preacher was still doing his thing. "The lord does not leave man to judge himself, for it is not man who judges, but god. My friends, do not judge or be judged. Only let the world be cleansed in baptismal flames so that the lord might judge for us. Those who are faithful will be saved his wrath!"

I still felt it. I felt inspired. Awed.

It was a false feeling, though. Knowing its source did not lessen the feeling, but I had some control over my actions. This was a control that I knew others here did not have, which was what made them dangerous. It made Henry Sharpe the most dangerous of them all.

According to Court, Henry Sharpe had followed Mr. Brown home the night of the murder, and another person had been there too. A woman. The same woman that everyone I talked to seemed to have seen, but nobody could identify. She was the real mystery.

I needed to get my bounty removed, which probably meant cracking the tainted dairy case and the whole business with the mysterious new sheriff.

I couldn't just let it go, though. I tensed, trying hard to blend in without completely losing myself in the orgy of faith. The congregation was being whipped into another frenzy. If the flames came again, I thought I might be able to duck outside.

The doors flew wide open with a thundering bang.

The congregation stopped and a murmur crept through the sanctuary. Suddenly, everybody turned around and looked at me. My heart raced and I realized that they were looking past me toward the back of the church. The dentist met my gaze but didn't say anything. A few of the bikers I had angered the previous night were there too, having apparently escaped the new sheriff. I cursed under my breath when I recognized the old lady who had shouted her hallelujah earlier. It was the same woman who had been to the station early in the morning to complain about Reverend Sharpe's unwanted proselytizing. I counted that as another law enforcement failure in my growing list.

They weren't paying attention to me, though.

"Got some business here," said a deep voice from outside the door. "I expect full cooperation."

I couldn't see who it was, but I knew. There was a slow, deliberate footstep and then another. The whole congregation seemed to hold its collective breath. Another step. I shifted so that the man closer to the door would mostly obscure me.

Then I saw him.

It was the man in black. He wore a three-piece black suit that was so dark that it sucked up all of the light around it. His hair was unnaturally black and slicked back with immaculate precision. His black goatee complemented it handsomely. A pair of solid mirrored coverings obscured his eyes, but his mouth was twisted into a sneer. There were no lines on his perfect skin—nothing to show that he'd ever smiled or frowned.

At first glance, his metal wasn't obvious. I envied that a little. Still, something smelled about him and his footsteps were far too heavy. He was an upscale modder but a modder nonetheless. By the cold look on his face, it seemed that compassion was part of the humanity he'd left behind. I had told Trish once that I could tell what a man was capable of. It was only a first impression, but I couldn't think of anything that this guy couldn't or wouldn't do.

"First off, where is Henry Sharpe?" Sheriff Balon Swayle spoke slowly, enunciating each word meticulously.

Every head in the crowd turned to the pulpit, including mine. Henry was gone.

The new sheriff frowned and the skin around his eyes hardened.

He cocked his head to one side and spoke to someone outside of my vision. "Go around the other side. Make sure they pick him up if he tries to get out."

"Yes, sir." It was Trish's voice, but it had an edge to it. I had plenty of experience hearing her annoyed voice, and this was it. What was going on there?

"Second," the sheriff paused like he was carefully considering his words. "The old sheriff is now a known criminal, charged with murder, theft, and terrorism. He will be found. If anyone here has information leading us to the man, then that person ought to bring forward that information. There is a considerable bounty."

There was a long pause. I sneaked a glance back at the crowd and noticed the dentist looking my direction. He gave me a nod and shifted uncomfortably. I wasn't sure if he would turn me in. He definitely recognized me.

There was nowhere for me to go. The crowd was pressing in. I hunkered down, trying to make myself blend in with the crowd and reveal my face to as few people as possible without looking like I had something to hide. That's when I saw the kid doing the same thing.

Francis Brown, the eight-year-old, had his flashing fancy eyes pointed in my direction. There was no expression on the child's face—not humor or passion or smugness. He simply stared. He knew who I was. For the life of me, I could not think of a reason he wouldn't turn me in.

Except, I had promised him I would catch his father's killer.

Sheriff Swayle was slowly making his way forward. The clumping of his footsteps formed a regular rhythm, punctuating the returning murmur of the crowd. I shifted, keeping most of my face hidden from the grim lawman.

Francis watched me with those flashing, emotionless eyes. I started to wonder if he really wanted me to catch the killer. If he knew that the killer was his own mother, he might be pretty motivated to stop me. After all, Billy Sharpe had been convinced that there was a witness. Sharpe had thought it was Ben, but it was possible that Francis was the one who had seen his father get killed.

The door was wide open, but there might have been a whole army just outside the door. Any movement toward it would certainly draw attention. The emergency exit was also too far away and the sheriff was watching it carefully. Henry had been lucky to duck out of the partially concealed door. I wouldn't get any such luck. I found it suspicious that the preacher would flee from the law like that. It made me think that maybe both the sheriff and the preacher knew a piece of the puzzle that I was missing. There wasn't time to think about it.

The sheriff was two thirds of the way up the aisle when he stopped. Ma Brown stood there.

The crowd's mood shifted. I felt it too. A sudden surge of fear set my heart racing again. My breathing sped up and a sheen of sweat formed on my brow.

"Ma'am." The sheriff nodded to the woman. It was the first personable thing he had done since arriving, and I was a little surprised to hear it. His voice softened when he spoke only to her. "Condolences."

The tension in the room ebbed just a little. Sheriff Swayle took another heavy step and then he stopped. I couldn't see who he was looking at, but he was right next to Ma Brown, so I prepared myself for what I suspected might be next.

"Benjamin Brown." The sheriff's voice was hard again.

My heart raced so hard it felt like it was tearing a hole in my chest. That urge to protect Ben surged again. My hand was on my pistol, unclipping the holster before I figured out what was happening.

"What the fuck is it to you?" Ben's voice made me smile a little. It was nice not being the focus of his unwarranted rage.

"You are under arrest as a member of the Cinco Armas gang."

I heard a quick scuffle. The lawman was likely grabbing the boy.

That's when the rage hit.

I knew it was coming. I had prepared myself, but still blind fury almost took me. My gun was out and I was halfway across the room before the light from the open door caught my eye.

In front of me was a mass of raging humanity. Every poor emo-chip-addled sap was trying to tear the sheriff apart. Two deputies, Johnson and another, were trying desperately to pull people off of the pile.

I stopped in the doorway and looked back. Wind whirled around the entry, sending sand into the air and causing my duster to crack like a whip. The raging mass of the congregation heaved upward, temporarily falling back from the sheriff. In no time, they fell back onto him, shoving him back and smashing him to the floor. In all of my days as a lawman, I had never seen such a mass of rage. It didn't matter how modded that sheriff was. He was going to die under that pile. He was likely to kill a number of innocents too.

Those folks were just victims, made insane by Ma Brown's surge of protective emotion. It wasn't just them that stopped me at the door, though. As much as I disliked the new sheriff I just couldn't let him go out like that.

There was no way I could get everyone's attention, but I didn't need to. All I needed was to get Ma Brown's attention. My gun was already in my hand. I pointed it skyward and fired one shot. The crack rang out like a cannon through the solid little bunker-church.

Everybody stopped.

There's nothing that grabs a mother's attention like a gunshot in closed quarters. For a moment, nothing moved. The mass of humanity froze and the deputies blinked at me, confused. The boy, Francis Brown, stood to one side. I only then noticed that he hadn't joined the fray.

Slowly, people began to peel themselves from the pile. Deputy Johnson was the first to speak.

"Boss, um, how did you get here?"

"Long story, Johnson. I'll explain back at the station."

"Right, well, about that..."

"Later," I said, taking a cautious step backward. "I have some work to do first."

Johnson drew his gun.

"Deputy," I said, eyeing the confused congregation behind him. "I am not interested in getting in a gunfight at this time. Please holster and we won't have any problems."

Johnson hesitated. "It's just, the new boss..."

I met Johnson's gaze, pleading silently for him to just let me go. It was his chance. He had to choose between his job and me. He knew me. He knew I wasn't guilty of anything. So really, he was choosing between following orders and following justice.

Balon Swayle faced us, but he looked like a freighter had hit him hard. He shook his head and tried to stand but stumbled back to one knee.

I took another step back. The tails of my coat flew behind me. The heavy door was next to me now, a sidestep might get me out of the line of fire, but Johnson had a bead on me. Our gazes were still locked, but I didn't like what I saw.

"You know me, Johnson. You got a duty to me, not this guy."

"The transfer was legit, J.D. Swayle is the new sheriff." His voice was gaining more certainty, more strength. I wracked my numb brain to find something that might have swayed him, but nothing came.

Swayle stood, recovering faster than I would have thought possible. He scanned the now cowering crowd with his shining eyes. He took a step, but nearly lost his balance when his knee buckled.

"Do what you need to do, Johnson, but remember, we're in this business for justice. We don't shoot fellas who haven't done anything wrong."

Johnson's hesitation was gone. "We do shoot fellas who are criminals and run from the law."

"That we do."

I brought my left arm up in front of me and dodged to the left. The slug from Johnson's pistol slammed into my hand, just where it would have hit my face. Johnson was trying to take me down just exactly how I had taught him to.

The force spun me off balance but didn't penetrate the army-grade black metal. It bought me enough time to get to the door, which I kicked hard. The heavy metal door slammed shut and I braced myself against it.

Their first attempt to get through nearly knocked me down. I was solid too. Johnson must have either had some pretty serious modifications that I didn't know about or the good sheriff was back on his feet. I knew I wouldn't last long.

The force hit again. The door slid a few inches, but I managed to force it back.

I scanned the area for something I could wedge under the door to buy myself enough time to get to my skidder. I tried to figure a way to jam the lock. Nothing came to me. My brain was still muddled from rage and adrenaline.

I couldn't think of any clever or violent solution, so I tried talking.

"Stop," I said. "Let's do this right, sheriff." I had given up on trying to talk to Johnson.

The force hit me again. This time I was ready for it. Almost. I stopped it but it felt a lot like a cheap flying sedan had hit me full on. The memory of what that felt like was still pretty fresh in my mind.

"Noon today," I spoke in calm, deep voice. I knew he could hear me. Nobody that modded ever neglected the ears. "The Brown Ranch. We'll settle it all."

The next hit was due but it didn't come.

"All of it. You, me, the Brown murder, the contamination. We'll settle it all at noon and only one of us is gonna walk away."

Silence. I started to suspect he'd just decided to go around the back entrance, but I wasn't sure how far away that put him. The emergency exit didn't just come out the back of the big concrete dome. It ran around through tunnels and came out somewhere around the hills. Maybe he didn't know that.

"All right," Balon said in his deep voice. "You'll have it, but you take what Deputy Contrisha's going to give you."

I turned away from the door to see Trish standing not three meters from me. I didn't know how long she'd been there, but I suspect it was long enough. She held a small device, like one a person would put in his ear. She tossed it to me and I caught it.

Once in, the little plug crackled with Sheriff Swayle's monotone voice. "I'll see you at noon, sheriff. You got three hours."

Trish's eyes met mine as I passed her on the way to the parking lot. I couldn't read what I saw there. She looked like she was intentionally keeping her expression blank. If I had to make a guess, I would have said she was apprehensive. I hadn't known her long, but she didn't seem the type to be overly indecisive. She seemed to be having trouble now. Maybe that's a natural thing when your old boss wants to kill your new one.

What I wasn't sure of was which of us was the new boss.

A belch of blue flame and I was cruising through the sky at a couple kilometers. High up, the air was cold and dry. It cleared my thoughts and let me consider fully what I had just signed up for.

I had really counted on Trish catching Henry Sharpe. He'd headed out the back door, after all. Somehow she didn't have him, which meant I might need to pick him up before noon. Ma Brown would be at the ranch, as would her boys. Billy Sharpe was out of reach. City folk had to deal with city folk as far as I was concerned.

Was he out of reach, though? The wheels were turning now. There was one man in the city that I thought I might be able to trust to bring Billy in. I figured if I could get all of the major players at the ranch, then maybe I could get everything nicely tied up before my showdown with the sheriff.

The clouds boiled below me. The lightning had stopped, but the storm was slowly building. To the west, a wall of darkness formed. My timing couldn't have been worse. The storm would hit in about three hours.

"J.D, what are you doing?" The voice was Trish's. For once, it didn't give me any sort of headache. In fact, I was glad to hear it.

"Your boss listening?"

"Probably."

"Can you make that not happen?"

"Probably not."

I grunted. It would have been better to keep the new lawman out of this, but my options were limited. "All right, you manage to get a hold of the good reverend?"

"Tracking him now."

Though I'd had very little to do with her training, I felt a bit of pride. She had managed to get to Henry before he escaped. Still, I had to wonder why she followed the same pattern of tracking instead of just capturing the target.

"Well, that's a nice plan, but I need him in now."

"Arrest him?"

"Bring him to the Brown Ranch. In cuffs, preferably."

"We'll see what we can do."

"I picked up a sample of Mr. Brown's blood yesterday. Can you take a closer look at that for me? The scan is in the system already. I'm also uploading a second sample for you to look at."

She paused. "I don't really work for you anymore, you know."

"Also." I hesitated, feeling a little embarrassed. "How do I work this earpiece? I might need to make a few calls to the city."

She sighed. "Just touch it and say a name. It'll talk you through any options."

"It hurts when I touch it."

"Don't," she paused. "Don't touch it so hard."

"But if I don't, it doesn't do anything."

There was an exasperated sigh on the line. "I'll ask again, J.D. What are you doing? What are you going to do?"

"There's someone I need to talk to before I go meet my maker."

Trish paused. "Where? Who?"

"Is it you who wants to know, or the good sheriff?"

"Maybe both."

"I'm going to the Dry Goat, if you must know. Might as well drink some liquid courage before the big date."

"You know," her voice had hardened. "You could have avoided all this. The new boss wouldn't have been able to take over if you had kept up with what was happening around you."

"Like what?"

"Like the widespread corruption threatening the food and power industries? Like the uncontrolled gangs riding all over your town? Like the murder that you were perfectly happy calling an accident when modern analytics easily picked it up as suspicious. Like drinking when you should have been investigating."

The line was heavy with silence.

I finally spoke. "I'm going to go get that drink then."

Chapter 16

"You could have saved me a lot of trouble, Lucy," I said.

The Dry Goat was packed. Either this was a preferred place of worship on a Sunday morning or the less fortunate residents of the city knew that this was the safest place to weather out the approaching storm. A rumbling low rhythm permeated the atmosphere, penetrating down into my bones.

Lucifer's black lips peeled back from his chrome teeth into a wicked smile. "But, then what reason would you have to drink?"

"Celebration?"

"Celebrating what? If your job is easy, what sense of accomplishment would you feel?" Lucifer pulled back, moving to the other end of the bar to help a couple of dark-skinned modders. When he returned, he was holding a small tray bearing two shot glasses and a small metal orb. He filled the glasses from an unlabeled bottle of a slick brownish liquid.

"I'm not here to drink," I said quietly.

"Yet drinks are here."

Those drinks looked so good. I licked my lips, tasting their desert dryness. I had been craving a drink since I'd been there the day before. Resisting hadn't done me much good back then, and there were some significant doubts that it would do me any good now.

"You putting this on my tab?"

"Way I hear it, you might not be good for it." His blue eyes sparkled with humor. "Let's just call this on the house, shall we?"

"Be a shame to turn down a free drink."

I picked up the metal marble and rolled it around in my fingers. It was warm to the touch and sparkled in the pulsing blue light. This was a stylish version of the same e-cuff tech that I used to stop criminals. Nannie blockers were often used to supplement drug and alcohol use in clubs like this. I'd been here before. I thumbed the orb open and clicked it into place on my metal arm.

My nerves were filled with a pleasant hum. The left side of my body became heavy and limp, but this wasn't the violent shock of an e-cuff. This was the stylish throb of a designer drug. What is a drug, after all, other than a way to disable a part of yourself? My eyes slid closed and the pulsing light and throbbing crowd faded into another world. The sharp static and then the silence in my ear told me the disabling signal of the designer anti-tech was working on my new earpiece.

With my senses clearer now, my nose detected the pungent odor of the liquor. It called to me. I figured I could just drink the first of two. I could still do what I'd come here for and then be on my way.

That wasn't how it worked, though. If I drank one, what reason would I have to not drink another? It wouldn't stop there either. It wouldn't take much to drop me on the floor. It never did.

I forced my eyes open.

The woman I had come here to see was sitting at a table all alone. I stood, stumbling a little from the dead weight of my disabled tech. It made me clumsy and made me look drunk, but I compensated and forced myself to move.

She glared at me as I awkwardly pulled out a chair and sat across from her.

There was a long silence. She had dark hair and smooth, tan skin. She was beautiful, in a way. Her eyes were a deep purple that doesn't happen in nature, though they looked otherwise unmodified. There was some redness around them. She'd been crying but was trying to conceal it as best as possible.

Finally, I broke the silence with the only thing I could think of to say to the woman. "Condolences."

She gave a weak smile.

"Can't be easy. Found a man you love and he's already married. Now he's dead and you can't even mourn properly."

I let that sit in the air for a while. Even with only a couple hours left, I didn't think there was any need to rush the conversation.

She spoke after a minute. "We were going to run away. Make a new life."

I nodded.

"Then he didn't show yesterday morning. I thought he'd backed out." She buried her face in her hands. "I was so mad at him."

"I know," I said. "I saw you that morning. That's how I knew it was you. I remembered seeing your anger and hurt and I just knew that you were the woman everyone was telling me about. It just made sense." I reached out and put my hand on her shoulder. "What happened the night before?"

She swallowed. "He got in a fight. He was roughed up pretty bad, but he was going to recover. His nannies were the best, you know. State of the art. He was healing already, so I drove him home."

"Did anyone see you?"

Her piercing purple eyes scanned my face for I don't know what. "Just the kid. I don't know what he was doing out there."

"Ben?"

She shook her head. "No. Francis, I think. The little one."

This new information took a little while to process. Something about the pulsing lights and throbbing music dulled the brain a little. If Francis was the one who saw this lady...

"What's your name?"

"Mina," she said. "Mina Honanie."

"Nice to meet you, Mina. Name's J.D. Crow."

She gave a weak smile. "Yes, I know. You are the sheriff."

"Was."

"Well, I am happy you have chosen to visit me, Mr. Crow."

"Why's that?"

"The crow is an omen of luck among the Hopi."

I smiled. I wished we had more time to talk. She reminded me of my mother; she held the same spark of life, the same sadness.

"They are revered for their intelligence," she said.

"Well," I said. "There doesn't seem to be a surplus of intelligence around here. I assumed the crow was an omen of death, since they eat carrion."

"So do a lot of things," she said. "Coyotes, rats, eagles."

I nodded. "Well, how would you like to help this old omen do something that might bring Mr. Brown's killer some justice?"

"I would be happy to help, sheriff." She leaned in close. "What are we doing?"

"We're going to break into the jail and set a few dozen criminals free."

There was a long pause and I suspected she might not be willing to help. Then she whispered so I could barely hear, "Sounds like fun."

Chapter 17

The station was not well guarded. Johnson was the only one there, the way I figured it. Trish was out tracking down the bad preacher, and the new sheriff was likely helping. Everyone else was likely on patrol or taking the day off.

Truth is, the new sheriff was probably tracking my every movement. I went through the trouble of sneaking out in the garbage, just in case there were eyes in the skies. Most likely, they just had a bead on my earpiece, but since I had disabled that they probably couldn't track it. They might assume I just wanted one last drink before going off to die.

They were wrong. I didn't want one last drink.

I wanted several.

My mind wanted to dwell on how good a drink would taste, but I forced myself to focus on the task at hand. I figured I had about twenty minutes before somebody started trying to track me down.

There were two ways into the station. There was a back entrance near the enclosed parking area, and there was the front entrance. The back was heavily guarded by some of the best tech in town. My understanding of such things was a little limited, but I understood that it boiled down to motion sensors with machine guns attached. Nothing to worry about if the system still thought I was sheriff, but not such a good day if it didn't.

Johnson was working the front desk. Since my last conversation with that beautiful man involved bullets, I figured a distraction was my best bet.

The rain had started. It was the sort of sideways mist that gets in your eyes no matter what you do. I hunched down and faced away from it, which helped a little, but water was leaking through my badly perforated duster. With a hat and a proper raincoat, Mina was better prepared. Still, she wasn't happy.

I waved Mina through the door. She gave me a worried look but went in.

Timing was critical.

In the war, stealth was a huge advantage. Tech, those days, had been developed to detect tech. Actually, tech had been designed for stealth, which other tech had been designed to detect. So, more tech was designed to hide from the stealth-detecting tech. You get the idea. Eventually, someone forgot to keep the thing that detected folks like myself. We naturals had a significant advantage in some very key situations. Early on, I was one of the best. People were usually pretty predictable. Just figure out what they're interested in and you know where they're going to be looking—and when. Don't be there.

That was twenty years ago. This situation was significantly different.

My advantage of stealth was gone the moment a wiki lasered off my left arm. Military grade black metal was the best stuff available and still is, but any creep with a metal detector could pick me out of a grassy field. Targeting systems would lock onto me like a dog onto steak. My military career was finished, but it didn't really die until the war was over. That's when I moved to Dead Oak. I thought I could do some good. I figured maybe a man like me could make life better for folks out there.

But things never got any better. They only got worse and the worse they got, the worse I felt.

There were no targeting systems up there in the front of the building. Mina was going to walk into the station with a complaint. For two minutes, she was going to describe to Johnson a man who had assaulted her the previous day. He had chromed teeth, modded legs, and spiked hair.

Johnson would tell her the man was in custody. He would insist but she wouldn't believe him. She would demand that something be done to track him down. She would claim that the man had been seen outside just minutes ago. She would yell. Johnson was a pretty professional guy, but he never did figure out how to deal with a woman yelling.

Two minutes passed. I listened closely at the door, expecting to hear what would happen next.

I did. Mina shouted. After two minutes, she turned up the pressure and I knew exactly how Johnson would react.

Thirty seconds later, I opened the door and entered the station.

I strode inside, shook the water from my oilskin duster, and tried to tip my nonexistent hat to Mina. My jaw involuntarily clenched. The lack of a decent hat was really starting to bother me. I'd need to get a new one if I survived, or possibly track down Ben to get mine back. I decided that's what I would do. I loved that hat.

Mina's eyes sparkled with amusement, probably at my hatless misery. She leaned against the counter like a woman bored with bureaucracy. Her braided hair still dripped a puddle on the undecorated concrete floor. When I didn't move for a moment, she gave me an impatient look and waved me through.

With my right hand braced against the counter, I vaulted over, landing softly on the other side. My boots were going to be too noisy, so I had left them by my skidder outside. Wet socks would likely plague me the rest of the day, but it was a small price to pay for a better chance of living.

There was a creak. The heavy metal door that separated the business end of the station from the jail slammed shut.

That was my chance.

I padded softly down the hall, glancing right as I passed the hallway to the jail. The door was closed, but I saw Johnson through a small window.

He didn't see me.

My first stop was my office.

I was halfway through a prayer before I remembered that my newfound faith was mostly an artificial product of some emotion-hijacking nannies. Luck would have to be on my side. If Swayle had added any security during his one day in the office, I would be in trouble. If he had even bothered to change the lock, I would have needed to start using brute strength to make my way around.

My office wasn't even locked. That was normal. In my twenty years there, I had only locked my office when I was inside it, as a matter of privacy. I pushed my way into the dark room and waited for my eyes to adjust.

The room was almost as I had left it. The desk display flickered alive, and greenish light played across the walls of the room. I cursed and flipped it back into standby, knocking over a slim metal flask as I did so. Standing it back up, I silently surveyed the rest of the room.

Embarrassment flushed my face as I remembered that the flask had been on the floor when I had left the previous morning. This must be why they knew I was an incompetent drunk on the job—a drunk, anyway. My incompetence probably spoke for itself when I botched the whole investigation with Trish. She was probably just there to watch for me to screw up. The city had sent her to undermine my position. Seemed like a crazy conspiracy theory to me.

I shook my head to clear all of that crap out of it.

What did it matter if she'd been sent to undermine me? I still had a grudging respect for her. No, I didn't like her, but she was damn good at her job.

The sound of movement in the hall sent me hiding behind the desk.

Long moments passed. My ears strained to hear Johnson's low timbre, but his voice was just too quiet.

He passed the door to my office and headed deeper into the station. I bit my lip. If this was my only chance to get into the jail, then I needed to move in a hurry, but I wasn't ready yet.

I moved to the wall safe in the corner. My thumb mashed up against the reader and I whispered the passcode, "Truth and justice for God and Texas."

The safe clicked open.

There was more in there than I could possibly carry.

Bullets were the first order. I grabbed a box of Red Number Fives and left the rest.

My eyes fell on a meter-long, triple-barrel, pulse-action Browning Blue Lightning.

E-cuffs were important, of course, so I stuffed a handful of those in my pocket.

The Browning Blue Lightning was the top of the line energy weapon back when I was in the army. One shot from one barrel of that weapon would stop a charging longhorn dead in its tracks. All three barrels would make it fairly likely nobody would eat steaks that night.

The first aid kit was probably a good idea, so I grabbed it. Bandages probably weren't going to do me any good after a gunfight, but you never knew what else could go bad.

There was no good reason to bring the Browning. Most likely, the entire event would be resolved peacefully, except for a short bit of violence in the end when either the new sheriff or I lost a whole lot of dignity and a life.

Time was running out. I pushed the safe closed silently, crept over to the door, and listened. Not a sound came from the hallway, but the whole station was filled with the quiet hiss of falling rain. Now was the time to move. If I hurried I could get over to the jail without being spotted by Johnson, thus simplifying my visit here.

I stood, stepped over to the safe, flung it open, grabbed the Browning, and slung it over my shoulder.

Better safe than sorry, my pa always told me.

Holding my breath, I crossed the hallway and ducked down the hall to the jail. Pausing there, I listened again. Nothing.

The door was closed and locked, but the system still accepted my thumbprint and voice. With an uncomfortably loud buzz, the door opened. I slipped through and pulled it most of the way closed behind me.

The jail was one of the best tools for an aspiring lawmaker. Most of the time, angry folks just need a little time to stop being angry, just like drunks need a little time to stop being drunk. The jail is a place where we store people who are having trouble abiding by the rules of our society. It is not a place of punishment. It is not a place to make people suffer so that they'll somehow realize that there's a big bad jail waiting for them so they should be nice. People in this part of the world just didn't think that way.

Sometimes, they needed a break.

The jail cells held some of the same tech that worked in the tiny e-cuffs. A rapidly oscillating signal pulsed through the air here. If my designer cuff hadn't already been disabling my electronics, then this signal would probably do it. Sure, there were ways to shield from it, but most folks didn't bother. There were ways to detect shielding, and the ever-escalating arms race just became meaningless at some point. Reinforced concrete and steel bars made up the decor in this place. The walls were painted white and the bars were orange. There were only six cells. At the far end of the hall was a seventh cell with its own tech and precautions. That was the interrogation room.

A dozen angry faces scowled in the cells, a mass of anger and humanity. None reacted when I entered the room, but they writhed and scratched blindly at the bars.

"Howdy, folks."

There was no response.

I shook my head. "You folks shouldn't be here," I said.

There was a switch by the door that controlled the anti-tech, and another one that controlled the individual cell doors. I flipped open the farthest door and walked over to its only resident.

It was Court. She was dirty and her fancy clothes were ruined. Two of her four arms had been clipped off just below the elbows. They stuck out of her ribcage like broken wings.

My face still stung from where she had clawed it. I seriously considered retribution. She would heal quickly, but it still didn't seem right to cause pain to such a beautiful and helpless creature. Plus, I was certain the scars from that wound would significantly increase the quality of my scowl. Call me vain if you want.

Court started when I touched her shoulder. Her face darted around like she was trying to see but couldn't. Those fully enhanced eyes and ears were doing her no good in this cell. She likely wouldn't even be able to walk, so I gently scooped her up in my one good arm and carried her to the interrogation room.

My foot slammed the door shut, and I dumped Court into a stout steel chair. She blinked a few times. Her eyes flashed to life and focused on me.

She smiled. "Oh and your beautiful face is all I could have hoped for."

I tried to keep the mixture of anger and distaste from showing on my face. "I've got a deal for you, miss."

"Well, I do believe I'm reformed, sheriff. You can just let me go, if you don't mind."

"We don't have much time."

"I believe I have a great deal of time. At least, that's what I'm led to believe. How long have we been in here? A day? A week?"

It had been less than half a day.

"A person loses track of time when her eyes and ears are gone," Court rambled. "My internal clock was even disabled. I don't believe I liked that very much. It gave me plenty of time to think, though. I decided a great many things."

"Look, we—"

"First of which is that I don't very much like you, Mr. Sheriff." Court lifted an arm in front of her face and wiggled her fingers. Her systems seemed to be restarting one by one. She flicked her fingers and those wicked sharp claws snapped out. Her eyes met mine, and her smile faded.

"Courtney," I started in the calmest tone I could manage.

She lunged.

Her butt got about half a meter from the seat before her balance shifted, and she fell backward with a solid thump. At her highest point she'd swiped her claws but fell short of my face.

She twisted and strained but couldn't get anywhere.

"Magnets," I said.

Her eyes met mine again. She was so full of rage and pain that I flinched and looked away. "It's not magnets, *pendejo.*"

I looked at her questioningly.

"You have me sitting on a damn gravity well."

"Plus magnets, right?"

She struggled again, bracing her hands against the arms of the chair and pushing down as hard as she could.

"I guess I always thought it was magnets." I felt the pull from across the room.

Losing a struggle against someone who doesn't really understand technology did not help me placate this woman, who practically worshipped the stuff. Changing topics seemed like it might be a good course of action, though I might have messed that up as well.

"Tell me about how you got caught," I said.

Court slumped back into the steel chair. "Some fucker blew up a bomb and brought down the law on my friends. That guy got away, but those of us whose skidders were blown up in the explosion had no way to escape."

I smiled. "The bomb you're referring to, is that the one you've been riding around town?"

"Possibly."

"This fucker you refer to, what makes you think he got away?"

"Cut the crap, sheriff. You could have just left, but you came back to ruin my gang and me. You wanted revenge and you got it."

"I did want revenge." I stepped closer to Court, too close to be safe if she decided to lash out again. "And it was wrong."

Her eyes narrowed and flashed with a greenish light. "You didn't really get away with it, did you?"

The conversation was taking way too long. "You want a deal or what?"

"Not really."

Our eyes met again. This time I held her hateful gaze until she blinked.

"What is the deal?"

"I'm lookin' to put together a posse."

She let out a sharp laugh. "You want to deputize me?"

I scowled. "I don't like the idea, but I need the backup. You get freedom, but you and your gang need to witness something."

She chuckled at some humor that I didn't quite get.

"I need you to witness a duel at noon today, that's all. No shooting, no fighting. Just witness the duel and make sure the results are honored. Make sure people know what went down."

Her chuckle developed worrisomely into a full-blown laugh. "Honor? You looking to me to honor a duel? Isn't there a judge in this town?"

"Duel's between the new sheriff and myself," I said. "And no, there's no judge. He quit years ago."

"No wonder the jail's so full." Her expression turned dead serious.

"We got a deal?"

She stared straight ahead and didn't answer.

I flipped a switch on the wall. "In a few minutes, the magnets will power down."

"Gravity well," she corrected me.

"Whatever. When that happens, walk out of here, free your friends, and meet me at the coordinates that I have written right here." I took out my glow cube with the coordinates of the Brown Ranch and showed it to her. "You can take my cruiser if you need a ride, but don't hurt anyone on your way out."

"What makes you think we'll come?"

I opened the heavy metal door and stepped out of the interrogation room, pulling the door most of the way shut after me. She was right. There wasn't a good reason for them to follow my orders. By all reasoning, they were the enemy. They were outlaws. There was a greater threat now, though. I wanted them to know about it, even if I wasn't around to help them fight it. Maybe they would get it, maybe they wouldn't.

All I said was, "Honor, Courtney. You'll be there for honor."

Her laughter echoed through the humming, sterile jail. It faded as I crossed over to the door, but by then I wasn't listening to it.

Something was wrong.

I scanned the hall. The prisoners were all still in their places. Only Court's cell was open and she had been alone. The others sat or sprawled out in their cells, rocking and moaning in their misery. The light above flickered a little, but the anti-tech seemed to be in good order. Then I spotted the problem.

The entrance to the jail closed.

Through the window, I saw a shadow of movement and my heart raced.

Johnson was just outside the jail.

I was going to have to make the call that I had been trying to avoid since I'd decided to sneak into the station. If Johnson saw me, it would be seconds before he had me down and locked up in a cell. The question was, could I trust him to let me go?

Of course, I knew I could trust him. He had been my right-hand man for years. I could trust him to enforce the law. I could trust him to fight for the freedom that people deserved, the freedom they'd earned. I could even trust him to do what was right in the face of terrible odds.

As much as I wanted to, I couldn't trust him to give a damn about me. He cared about his job and he was loyal to the sheriff.

I wasn't sheriff anymore.

I padded silently up to the door, ducking low to keep out of view as much as possible. Johnson wasn't looking in, though.

My nostrils flared and I set my jaw, ready for action.

With my right hand, I slowly reached for the door handle. I closed my fingers around it and braced myself.

I turned the handle and pulled. In one quick motion, I threw the door open and kicked the back of Johnson's knee. Hard.

He dropped like a sack and gave a somewhat comical shout of surprise. With my only functioning hand, I grabbed his shirt and dragged him back into the jail.

Johnson shuddered. The anti-tech was affecting him, so he would lose most of his enhanced strength.

I stood.

My foot came down hard on Johnson's chiseled face. I kicked again and again, but without my boots the savage kicks did little real harm.

Twice he tried to say something between kicks. Once he tried to stand before being throttled back to the ground.

Then he caught my foot and twisted it.

It was my turn to hit the floor. My face whacked against the concrete, sending lights flashing in front of my eyes. My wounds opened and blood smeared across the cold concrete. Johnson kept hold of my foot, standing and twisting my knee into an awkward angle. With his formidable strength, Johnson held my lower half in the air.

I tried to talk but my words came out as a mumble, since my face was smashed into the concrete.

"What?" Johnson said.

I mumbled again. He applied more pressure. My knee was strained and pain ripped through my leg.

"What did you say? Just come quietly, sir. I don't want to hurt you." He shifted a little and eased up on the knee.

It was all I needed. My face was no longer planted on the cold slick concrete, and I had just enough freedom of movement to angle my body correctly.

"Johnson," I said, my voice coming out slowly and quietly. "I'm sorry about this."

Without unholstering my Smith and Wesson, I pulled the trigger. The deafening boom of the weapon shattered the humming peace of the jail, shocking all of the prisoners into chaos. Johnson's head snapped back.

Johnson dropped my lower half and fell stiffly backward onto the floor. Dead or unconscious, he wasn't moving any time soon. I stayed down and pulled myself over to a wall. Prisoners shouted and grabbed through the bars at anything they could reach. One pulled at my coat, but I yanked it free. A line of blood started to soak through my pants, and I realized that the bullet had grazed my leg before hitting Johnson.

It stung but I figured it was the least of my problems.

The body on the floor shifted. He was still alive. By the awkward hang of his jaw I figured I had finally managed to mess up his beautiful face, probably broke his jaw. This made me feel worse than I had about anything I had done already. Johnson didn't deserve this sort of treatment.

I forced myself to stand. The wound in my leg was deep, but not as bad as it could have been. Johnson was heavy. I grabbed him with my one good arm and dragged him into the interrogation chamber. Court was there, still trying to stand. I mashed the controls on the wall and turned the magnets all the way off.

She stood slowly and stared at me with what looked like a mixture of hatred and superiority. Distaste, maybe.

I ignored her and placed Johnson on the chair. With the magnets back on, he wouldn't be able to stop me. Once the door was closed, though, the anti-tech wouldn't affect him. His nannies would be able to start healing that ruined face. I reached down and did my best to set his broken and dislocated jaw, wincing at the sickening pop it made as I forced it back in place. I ran my fingers through his hair, feeling the warmth radiating from his body. Would he ever forgive me for what I'd done to him? The question bothered me, but in all fairness he had shot at me first.

The cigarettes in his front pocket were practically calling out to me, so I borrowed the pack and lit one. I brushed past Court in a cloud of smoke and gunpowder. She might have finally come to respect me. She might have been fixing to kill me. I didn't give a damn. I walked out of the jail and found Mina in the lobby.

She shook nervously. "What happened?"

"Things got a little rough, but he'll live."

Mina nodded and the two of us left the station, heading over to where I'd left my skidder and my boots. Rain was soaking everything now, blasting sideways through the empty streets. "We done, then, sheriff?"

"Yeah," I said, slipping my soaked feet into my boots. "Just stay safe in the storm."

"You, too." Her voice was almost a whisper. She ran to the Dry Goat, where she had been sheltering before I'd dragged her out into the storm. Lightning cracked across the sky, lighting up the boiling, dark clouds.

"Not planning on it," I said under my breath.

Seconds later. I was rocketing though the turbulent sky, lightning flashing all around me.

Chapter 18

Frigid air filled my lungs a hundred meters above the rolling white clouds. They looked so harmless from above, like a fluffy avalanche of cotton balls tumbling to the east. To the west I could see the wall approaching. We would have time, I estimated, but just barely.

A wave of dizziness drifted over me. Maybe it was the lack of oxygen or maybe it was the way the clouds moved below me. It was hard to orient myself up there. I gripped my Smith and Wesson hard in my left hand.

I was nervous. My heart beat too fast and my right hand shook as I loaded the weapon. It had been that way since I had re-enabled my tech. Was it my own fear of death that made me nervous? Were Ma Brown's emotions being pushed down on me? Maybe it was my fear of not being in control of my own emotions. If I lost control now, I was bound to make a mistake.

For instance, I couldn't decide whether or not I should really be using the Red Number Fives.

Red Number Fives were invented by a man named Ernest Redd near the end of the Civil War. They were a solution to the escalating arms race between armor and bullets. Red Number Fives would punch through the armored hull of a tank if you hit it straight on. Someone had explained it to me years ago. The bullets came with a nano-pulse sheath to disable powered shielding. Also, there was something to do with a plasma core and black metal tip. I understood the bit about black metal. It'll punch through armored skin without any trouble at all. It'll kill pretty much anyone it hits.

That's why I never used them before.

I rolled one of the crimson bullets in my fingers and watched the reflections of the storm in its surface. Did I really want to kill Sheriff Swayle? When I thought about it, my brain got all tangled up. I hated the guy for everything he'd done to me. It was wrong how he'd sent the bounty hunters after me. It was horrible how he had treated the Cinco Armas, even if they were a bunch of borderline criminals.

Yet the sheriff had agreed to settle our differences like men. I had to respect the man for that. Still, it wouldn't be right for me to use non-lethal bullets in a duel. That would be dishonoring the tradition.

I finished loading the gun with specials and took another moment to breath in the icy, thin air.

This was it. It was time to get everything taken care of. I pushed the bike forward and rocketed down into the boiling clouds.

The world flared around me as lightning struck my skidder the instant I entered the cloud.

Next thing I knew, I was falling without a ride. Pain tore through my body, like every muscle was struggling to fight against itself.

I shook my head and looked around. Air screamed in my ears and lightning flashed all around. The wet air was charged. It felt like it might crack me once again before long.

The sky opened up below me.

I could see it all from up here. Straight below me, the Brown Ranch sprawled out for kilometers. The black windmill fields pulsed greedily in the wind. Spinning below was my skidder. The bike had shut down and was in free fall just like me.

An eerie calm fell over me. God in his might had struck me down with lightning. I wasn't dead yet, but I would be. Soon. He was telling me once more that my time was done.

The Almighty should have known that I would not take such a subtle hint.

My duster had loops that were attached to my legs so that it wouldn't flap too much in the wind. I spread my legs and angled myself downward. I felt like a damn flying squirrel. I approached the spinning skidder.

Thunder cracked and the sky lit up again. In the flash of light, I spotted something else falling just above me. The Browning was spinning farther away and out of reach.

The skidder was close now. The bike was almost within reach, but it was spinning so fast I wasn't sure I could hold on. I shoved my metallic hand into the spinning vehicle to slow it down before attempting to grab it with my good hand.

It worked but the force spun me around and sent me tumbling away. I caught the air with my coat again and tried to reorient myself.

The world grew closer. I could make out the tiny ranch house and barn. Figures moved around down there, and I could make out a cluster of activity.

With my black metal hand, I grabbed at the bike.

This time it worked. My three fingers clamped on hard and I was able to pull myself into the seat.

I clamped my left hand on hard, not wanting to lose control again. With my other hand I started fiddling with the controls. The antigrav wasn't working at all. Normal controls were completely lost.

I set the jets to point straight down and cranked the power all the way up.

My hand hovered over the button.

Raindrops fell straight down all around me. I looked at one, focused on it falling in its little, round perfection. The drop was just in front of my face, falling at the exact same speed. I marveled at its beauty. Nature had made this perfect beauty. Nature had made millions of them and sent them to the dry land to give us life. In return, we had given back nothing.

I pounded the button and fired the jets. At the same instant, lightning lit up the world and thunder cracked through the sky. Blue flames fired straight down and my gut felt like it was going with it. My free fall ended abruptly and I slowed.

The skidder hit the ground hard, sending a shockwave up through my spine.

I stood from the crash, somehow mostly uninjured. My heart was pounding on the walls of my chest like it was trying to punch its way free. Looking around, I determined that I was behind the house, but I'd drifted off target by a kilometer. Windmills buzzed all around me.

It was nearly noon. I stood and ran.

I slowed to a walk and gasped for breath once I was close. As I left the last line of windmills I saw something I was extremely happy to see.

It was my hat.

Ben sat behind the house feeding the baby Toby from a bottle. The chameleon poncho was draped over the two of them, protecting and partially hiding them both. I walked up to him and held out my hand.

His eyes narrowed, but he knew what I wanted. He took off the hat and handed it to me.

"I was just keeping it warm for you."

"I bet."

"Wasn't sure you were coming back."

"I wasn't sure either."

"You gonna quit fucking this up?"

I put on my hat. A black bird circled low, silhouetted by the flashing sky. When it landed on the roof of the house, I could see that it was a crow. It was a symbol of luck. It was a good omen.

"Yes, son. I do believe I am."

The rain stopped.

There was no wind.

I walked around the side of the house to see what waited for me. It was more than I expected and everything I hoped. Murderers and madmen waited with lawmen and outlaws. Nearly the entire congregation had also decided to attend. However this turned out, there would be plenty of witnesses.

The time had come to sort the good from the bad.

Chapter 19

Everything went silent. Lazy wisps of steam drifted up from the hot, wet ground. In the distance, a dark wall stretched from field to sky. Yellow light flickered in its midst.

The Cinco Armas gang floated in a combination of skidders and cruisers in the middle ground between the barn and the house. The tension with which they gripped the controls of their vehicles suggested they might bolt at any second. All together, they formed a semicircle with the line between the barn and the house as the dividing border. From the backseat of what used to be my own cruiser, Court alone was relaxed, gazing down at us with a look of mild contempt.

Opposite the swarm of outlaws was a much smaller contingent representing law and order. On the ground, I saw Trish in her cruiser. The Reverend Sharpe looked like he had been bolted to the backseat. He looked upset for reasons I could only guess.

Behind Trish, near the house, there was a cluster of townsfolk and ranchers, many of whom I recognized. The dentist Dr. Cornsley was there, hanging close and twisting his hands together in apparent nervous agitation. Ma Brown was there, of course. She scowled at me. It was a frozen kind of scowl that melted not one bit when I met her gaze and tipped my hat. The boy, Francis, was clinging to her hip. Some of the others from the good reverend's congregation had showed up. Whether they were there to protest the arrest of their reverend or to just visit Ma Brown, I did not know. Maybe they were only there to see the good show I was fixing to put on.

Near the house was a vehicle I did not recognize. It was a truck, a freight hauler with Goodwin Dairy printed on the side. It floated a few feet up. On the ground in front of it were two men I recognized. The first was Jenkins from Goodwin Dairy. I had given him a call after the little incident at the church. I figured he might want to be here for this. Next to him, cuffed and tied, was shiny-haired Billy Sharpe.

I tipped my hat to Jenkins and then turned to face the sheriff.

"'Mornin', sheriff," I said.

"'Mornin'."

"You been in one of these before, son?"

"I'll do what I need to do." His dark eyes were on my metal hand. I figured he thought that was the biggest threat.

I brushed back the coat on my right side, revealing the Smith and Wesson 500 in its holster. It was unclipped. The safety was off.

A wave of lethargy swept over me, making my arms feel heavy and my neck stiff. This was hopelessness and I knew it wasn't mine. It was a product of the machines in my blood. A glance over at Ma Brown told me she was feeling pretty much the same. I wiggled my fingers and shook the slowness out of them. A good lawman knows what to do with out-of-control emotions. A good lawman ignores them.

Not that I was still a good lawman. At that point, I'd had enough of the law. I was there to clear my name or die trying. If I had to die, I figured it might as well be in front of everyone so they'd know what sort of lawman they had as my replacement.

"You see that crow up there?" I said, indicating the black bird that was still perched up on the roof.

He nodded.

"When that bird flies, we shoot."

The sheriff pushed back his coat, revealing a weapon in its holster. It was something fancy—something made of shiny metal with a long barrel and a black cylinder that spun. It reminded me of Court's weapon, only bigger.

"That a needler?"

He nodded, keeping his eyes on the crow.

"Trish," I spoke a little louder than needed. "What'd you say killed Sam yesterday?"

"Needles." She was speaking a little louder than necessary too. A ripple of movement passed through the Cinco Armas members.

"Care to explain, sheriff?" I said.

There was a long pause. "I began watching Deputy Chin's vid feed when I had such trouble locating you. I saw the incompetence and brutality with which you interviewed that gangster, but I also saw his guilt. I could not allow him to walk free."

"He wasn't guilty."

"He ran when I tried to arrest him. He was going to fight."

"He warned Ben of the danger." I said. "What you did was you murdered him."

The sheriff's voice dropped to a growl. "He was conspiring against the people of the city. He had to be stopped. They all need to be stopped."

"They all?"

"They all. You all. You outlanders think you got all the power, just because you control all the food. You people think there's nothing wrong with making a play for control of the city with your emo nannies and iron grip on our power supply." He looked around at everyone watching. "We've had enough of it! We don't want a war, but we've had enough!"

"So you murdered the kid."

"I killed one criminal."

"Speaking of murder," I said, turning to Trish. "You ever run that blood scan on Mr. Brown?"

"Checked out normal, except—"

"Nannies?"

"Yup."

"Special ones, right? Nonstandard."

"Yup. Aggressive. Bovine-grade."

A low rumble of thunder swept across the field. The crow spread its wings and flexed a few times. It shifted from one foot to the other.

I looked at Ma Brown. Francis was still clinging to her. His face was buried in her side. Her square jaw was set hard and her eyes were focused right at me. My heart raced and I felt a pressure on my lungs. The hopelessness was swept away under a flow of unplaced anger. Behind Ma Brown I saw the dentist, Dr. Cornsley, pick something up off the ground. I couldn't see what it was. He looked just as angry as her. This was going to get ugly fast.

"Mrs. Brown," I said. "You wanna tell us a story about what happened that night or do you want me to take a stab at it?"

Her face hardened even more, which I didn't even think was possible.

"Well, I'll give it a shot and you let me know if I'm close." I glanced up at the crow again. The sheriff was still staring it down, but it hadn't moved. I figured I'd know when it did.

"That night, Dan showed up smelling of drink, just like you said, but he wasn't alone." I paused as a flash of lightning set off a nearly deafening crack of thunder. "He brought a friend. A lady friend, but he told you there wasn't nothin' going on."

I faltered for a second when I saw what the dentist had picked up. It was my Browning. By the look of it, he'd managed to activate the power cells.

"Now," I continued, "whether or not you believed him, I don't know. I think you wanted to believe him, though. That's when the good Reverend showed up and offered to help."

Reverend Sharpe pulled at his bonds but was unable to move. "I have done nothing wrong in the eyes of the lord," he said in a quiet voice. He turned his eyes my way. "It is he who wants to ruin our good work, Mrs. Brown."

The grip on my chest tightened.

"That might be true, but listen to my story for a moment." I stole another glance at the crow. It was making me nervous, but I wanted to get this out before the sheriff and I ended things. "Reverend, you offered Mr. Brown a baptism knowing full well what would happen. Cleansed of his sins and all that, right?"

The elder Sharpe nodded.

"Thing is, I've seen how you baptize. You use fire for show and a special ingredient that I bet most folks in your church don't know about. You use the emo chip embedded in your most faithful follower to force faith upon anyone who has those particular nannies in their system. Nannies they get from drinking contaminated milk."

"I only show them the truth, that they might be saved."

"You'd like to save more than just us, though. Sheriff Swayle's theory is right, isn't it?" I nodded to Jenkins. "Your son put together a pretty nice distribution network in Austin, skirting around the regulations that Big Milk usually has in place. How many faithful would you say you've made?"

"Not enough."

"I suppose that's one way to look at it." My breathing was shallow. Sweat beaded on my brow and I felt a chill.

The reverend's eyes were downcast. He didn't say a word.

"The interesting part about this faithful baptism of yours is that people tend to say what's on their minds, don't they? Mrs. Brown, your husband told all, didn't he?"

She took a step forward, but Trish hopped out of her cruiser and blocked her. I was struggling to pull air into my lungs. My heart was racing even faster than it had at the church. There was pain, sharp pain. I blinked hard a couple times, trying to clear my vision.

"J.D.," Trish said. "What's going on?"

"Brown," I said. "She's proving a point. With enough nannies. She can kill a person. Just by hating them hard enough." I gasped for air.

Trish turned to Ma Brown. "Stop it, Mrs. Brown."

She didn't stop.

"You don't need to do this. You can't win if you kill him!"

I dropped to a knee. My vision was turning black around the edges. I couldn't talk. I wanted to tell them the rest. I needed to tell them about how Ma Brown was not a murderer. She was only the weapon.

"Well, hell," said Trish. She stepped forward and cracked Ma Brown on the back of the head hard. Ma Brown collapsed but so did I.

My focus shifted. I looked away from Ma Brown and the strangely emotionless Francis kneeling over her. There were tears in the eyes of his expressionless face.

The pulsing windmills in the background drew me in with their hypnotic pull. They still spun. The closest ones spun slowly in the dead air. Farther away, blades spun like saws cutting madly at the sky.

Trish glared at Ma Brown's followers. "Don't move." The dentist dropped the Browning and put up his hands. He looked confused as he drifted backward into the crowd.

Trish ran over to me. "J.D, get up. You're in a gunfight, remember?"

I coughed a little, managed to pull in a little air. My heart raced. My lungs felt like they were full of hot lead. Ma Brown was out cold, but her last E-chip signal seemed to still be in full force.

In the distance, the line of speeding windmills was rapidly approaching. The next wave of the storm was fixing to hit.

"Fine." Trish stood. "I'm standing in for J.D."

I shook my head but couldn't talk. Pain like liquid fire had spread from my chest to my arm, down to my fingers. Fighting the blackness that was threatening to take me, I forced my hand into my pocket, fumbling with the e-cuffs.

The sheriff finally pulled his eyes from the crow. "No need to do that, deputy. You'll just get yourself killed."

"Then don't shoot me. Walk away."

"Gotta be done. We need this, Contrisha. The city needs us out here. They need us to have the respect of these folks, so we can keep the peace."

"No, Balon. They don't need us. J.D. did just fine."

The sheriff's expression grew grave. "He didn't. He never would have cracked that milk conspiracy. You said yourself he wasn't even going to go after the murderer. Didn't even think it was a murder."

"He would have figured it out."

"Maybe."

"He would." She didn't sound so sure.

The crow flexed its wings again. I was beginning to suspect that the bird knew the rules to our little arrangement and was just toying with us. The line of

190

spinning windmills was close now, only a couple hundred meters from the edge of the field. I managed to pull in another breath, but I felt like my face was fixing to turn purple. My heart still felt like a little molten ball of fire. Seconds passed.

Far afield I saw another line in the windmills. Slowly, starting with the windmills farther upwind, they were shutting down. The arms stopped and folded themselves downward. They only did that when hurricane-force winds were about to hit.

The sheriff shook his head. "I have to do it," he said as he turned back to stare at the bird. "The people need to see strength. They need to see what we're willing to do to maintain the peace. It has to be this way or there's going to be another civil war."

Trish nodded. "That why you killed Sam? Is that why you rounded up Cinco Armas whether or not they were guilty of anything?"

"I do what needs to be done."

"So do I."

The stubborn crow took off like a shot into the air.

There was a single gunshot. I looked to see Trish standing with steel in her eyes and smoke rising from her gun. Swayle dropped.

With my fumbling fingers, I finally gripped one of the e-cuffs and slammed it onto my metal arm. The familiar jolt racked my body and I convulsed hard.

The first blast of wind hit hard. People stumbled where they stood. Cinco Armas and Jenkins all started to have trouble controlling their vehicles. A half-dozen Cinco Armas landed. The rest flew away. Jenkins parked his freighter next to the house and started trying to pull the young Sharpe out.

Reverend Sharpe somehow pulled free of Trish's cruiser and bolted for the house. Others from his flock followed.

Ma Brown sat up straight.

She grabbed the Browning.

Her eyes were filled with a rage that I didn't share. With the nannies in my blood disabled by the e-cuff, my emotions were once again my own. They were far from calm.

She raised her weapon.

Francis shouted. Fear covered his face. He pulled at her, even grabbed the weapon for a second before she forced him back.

My muscles still screamed but I rolled myself to one side and drew my weapon.

"He got what he had comin'!" Ma Brown pointed the Browning at me. "The good lord struck him down and ain't no way you going to take my family!"

I saw madness in her eyes—madness and hatred and fear. In that split-second, I saw she would do it. She would kill me, Trish, and Sheriff Swayle if she needed.

I shot her.

I don't know if I still thought I had regular bullets loaded. Maybe I didn't think about it. Maybe I didn't care. It might have happened so fast that it just wouldn't have mattered. Thinking back on it, I can't say I'd have acted any different if I'd been thinking more clearly. It was her or me.

Lightning flashed across the sky as I pulled the trigger. Everything lit up and the image of Ma Brown's exploding neck was burned into my eyes.

She dropped.

Francis stood. He stared at me and his face twisted into a mask of rage.

Then he ran.

Near the house, chaos had taken over. The Sharpes had both freed themselves. Jenkins was on the ground with

Billy Sharpe's boot on his neck and a gun to his head. A dozen onlookers, Cinco Armas and otherwise, were crushing their way into the house. These were people who understood the danger of a true megastorm.

Wind tore at me as I stood, but I knew that wasn't going to be the worst of it. The windmills at the edge of the field shut down. The worst was seconds away.

"I guess you're the sheriff again, boss." Trish was next to me. Behind her I saw Swayle in a heap on the ground. The upper half of the man's cranium was conspicuously missing.

I looked at the chaos around the house. There was shouting but I couldn't make out the words. Billy Sharpe was waving a gun around like a madman, threatening punks and regular folk alike. Reverend sharp ducked into the house. Some of the skidders farther afield hadn't been properly locked down, and the wind picked up one of them, sending it straight for the mass of people. Something had to be done fast.

Francis was still running for the barn, but he wasn't going to make it.

My first thought was to take charge, shout orders, and be the line of justice that I had been for so long. I could command these people. With a gun and a booming voice, I could bring order in the face of chaos.

The dentist made a running tackle at Billy, knocking the weapon free and somehow managing to bite the sleazy merchant in the process. Blood gushed from the man's arm and covered the dentist in a grisly image that I believed would keep me from my regular dental cleaning for a good long while.

Bea, the old lady who'd been harassing poor Johnson just the day before, yanked a spiked gangster down to the ground just as an errant skidder blasted past. The flare from its burner sent black smoke trailing from her Sunday best, but she saved the kid from almost certain injury.

Court was using my cruiser to block the wind and create a narrow path for people to make their way into the house.

"No, Ma'am," I said to Trish, holstering my weapon. "I believe the law puts you in charge. I'm just a well-meaning citizen. You're the only deputy on scene."

She didn't pause for a second. "Then get your ass in gear, citizen." She pointed at Francis, who was only about half of the way to the barn. "Save that kid. I'll take care of the Sharpes."

I ran.

I thumbed the e-cuff as I went, letting it drop to the ground. Ma Brown's transmitting days were over, so I figured I was safe. We were running straight into the wind, so I lowered my head and fought hard to catch up. Strength came back to the metal fast, and I put on a burst of speed by grabbing the ground and launching myself forward.

The second wall of wind hit the boy before it hit me. It lifted him into the air and he tumbled back several meters.

As he sat up, I caught him, grabbing his leg with my metal hand, and flung him over my shoulder.

He fought, kicking and hitting and screaming. He bit my ear, but I didn't let go.

It was all I could do to fight the storm. Grit and water blasted my skin and nearly pushed me back. Running toward the barn felt like climbing a mountain. My body was leaned so hard into the wind that when the wind shifted I almost toppled right over.

The windmills were no longer visible. The air filled with rain and dirt and chickens. A skidder crashed past me. The wall of wind rotated. I could just barely make out the looming shape of the barn in front of me.

I squinted my eyes against the storm.

The kid shouted at me, but I ignored it. He stopped hitting. I remember trying to hold onto him as hard as I could. No way was I going to let the kid go. I was the only one who could stop that storm from carrying him away.

With a renewed determination, I forced myself forward. I ran on two feet and one hand now, keeping low so the wind wouldn't sweep me away. I was nearly blind from the dust and debris and mud.

Twenty meters from the barn another strong gust hit. It lifted us up and dropped us a couple meters to the left. I kept going.

Ten meters away, the wind changed drastically. The barn was acting like a breaker, slowing the wind and causing it to whip around seemingly at random. When I reached the barn I turned to see the rotating twister between the house and us. The funnel bounced across the ground, tearing the earth wherever it went.

I wrenched the door open and dove inside.

I tossed the kid to the floor.

The air in the barn was oddly still. It was heavy with the musk of the beasts inside, filled with their nervousness. Despite the rapidly dropping temperature outside, it was hot inside the barn.

There was a noise from the floor, a sort of whimper.

I couldn't see anything.

"You all right, kid?" I spoke quietly in a voice that I hoped hid my sense of guilt. I had killed the kid's mother.

Still, he cried.

"Look, Francis." I closed my eyes. They were still full of grit from outside. "Frank, I mean. Your ma. I didn't have a choice."

The crying stopped. I started to think that what I'd said had maybe made a difference, but something told me I was wrong. Like an idiot, I kept talking.

"She didn't kill your pa. It was that Sharpe guy. He was using her like a weapon. She knew it but she couldn't help it any more than you can help hating me right now. You'll understand some day."

My vision was starting to adjust. Black shapes started to form in the dark barn. The wind still screamed outside, but there was no evidence of it inside. The boy was still sitting curled up against the wall.

"I wish it hadn't gone down like that, son," I said.

I saw his eyes flash in the darkness. They were red and angry. I turned my back to him, letting my eyes focus on the hulking shapes of the longhorns. I started to walk. My muscles still ached, but the run had stretched most of the pain out of them.

"We just gotta wait out this storm here. Trish will take care of what needs to be done at the house, and those Sharpe fellas will find some justice. Just you wait, kid. The world needs strong people to bring justice into it and there ain't nobody stronger than Trish."

More silence from Francis. It seemed strange. For some reason I'd expected more. I turned back to him. My eyes had finally adjusted to the darkness.

That's when I noticed his leg.

Francis was glaring up at me with eyes that sparked red. His leg was twisted under him, crushed where I'd been holding him in the storm.

I had held him too hard. I tried to keep him safe and in doing it I had hurt him. Crushed him. I looked down at my hideous metal hand.

It was a tool of war. I was a tool of war, all sharp edges and blunt force.

I slumped down next to the kid and buried my face in my one good hand.

"I'm sorry, kid," I said. "I'm sorry."

Chapter 20

In a way, I'm responsible for everything that kid ever did. That day, despite my best intentions, I taught him that those who love you aren't always good people. I taught him that they don't always stick around when you need them. I taught him that even lawmen don't keep their word and there's nobody in the world that you can trust. He learned that people are weapons. I taught him that life is hard, and when it's hardest, killing is the solution.

I'll never forget that day, and I'll always regret it.

For the life of me, I have never been able to figure out what I could have done better.

Maybe the kid was already a monster. He had always been strange, emotionless, and distant. What he went on to do made me think that he could have been saved. There was a good kid in there. He could have been a good man.

Once the storm had passed, we got some medical help for the kid. With the help of an increasingly heroic Ben, Trish managed to subdue the Sharpes. I never doubted that she would. Jenkins survived, which actually did surprise me a little. The following day, Trish, Jenkins, and I met up at the Dry Goat to discuss the events over some strong drink.

"We've cleared your name, J.D." Trish always liked to start with business. I preferred to start with drink. "You could come back as sheriff now, if that's what you'd like."

I finished my drink and signaled for another. The aggressive nannies were extremely efficient at purging poisons from blood, so I wanted to keep ahead of them. I had resisted the urge to disable them completely. "Someone ought to teach you how to properly hog-tie an outlaw." I turned to Jenkins. "You too, city boy."

He smiled. "I suppose there's quite a bit someone of your advanced years could teach a person."

I began by demonstrating my best scowl.

"So, are you back?" Trish asked.

"I don't think so. Not yet, anyway," I remembered something that had been bothering me. "How is Johnson?"

"Not good." Trish paused for a while, considering what to say next. "You messed him up pretty good. I think he'll heal, but it's pretty painful."

Lucifer delivered the next drink, which I drained quickly. By the time I slammed down the glass, he had poured another. It seemed a pretty sad state of affairs, when the guy who knows you best is a bartender named Lucifer.

Another change in topic was in order. "What about the Browns? What's going to happen there?"

"Well," Jenkins said, "we're going to look into reinstating their license to sell through Goodwin—once their milk is clear of nannies, that is."

"Ben has contacted an older brother named Jason," said Trish. "Say's they're going to run the farm together, but I wouldn't be surprised if Jason went and sold it."

"Francis?"

"The kid won't speak to anyone. They'll get his leg fixed up, mostly."

"Kid's not right in the head," I said. "When he was in the barn he was in pain, but he just shut it off. He shut down his feelings like a switch. Kid shouldn't be able to do that."

"Neural boosters," said Jenkins. "They let people enhance some kinds of mental processing, but sometimes people can use them to completely shut down other parts of their brains. It must have been something he learned to do to protect himself against the emo nannies."

"Sounds bad."

"Well, it's good and bad. It means he didn't feel as much pain. I've never heard of someone putting them in a kid that young."

Trish bit her lip. "I think things had been hard for the Browns for a long time before Daniel was murdered."

She shifted in her chair and took a tiny sip of her drink. It was strong stuff. Texas whisky burned as it went down, and I could tell she wasn't used to it. She turned to me. "How long are you going to be gone?"

I indicated the pack that I had brought with me and was now sitting in a lump on the floor. "Maybe a year. Got some traveling to do. I'm going to live with a friend for a while, maybe pick up a few more tricks."

Trish smiled, "You have a friend?"

Jenkins smiled too. I couldn't figure what exactly was amusing about the idea of me having a friend.

"Let's just call her an acquaintance."

"A lady acquaintance?" Trish's smile broadened.

"Yes. A lady acquaintance." The alcohol seemed like it was finally winning the fight against those nannies. Despite myself I broke into a genuine grin. "Maybe a lady friend, but just in the friend sort of way."

"Of course," Trish said.

Just then, Mina walked in. I waved her over to our table and she nervously accepted.

"Mina," I said, "this is Jenkins and Trish."

Trish stood and shook Mina's hand.

I nodded. "Mina is Hopi. She agreed to take me on and teach me their ways."

Mina said, "They've agreed to have you, but it's not an easy life."

"Don't expect it to be."

"We live off of the land. Subsistence farming, hunting, that sort of thing. Most of the old ways are forgotten but we do our best."

Jenkins said, "Sounds like less work than running an enormous ranch like the Browns."

"It's not. And if we have a bad year, people can starve."

"That's why you wanted out?"

"It was a hard year. Next will be harder."

"Maybe I can help."

Mina scanned around the tavern. She bit her lip. The place must have been uncomfortable for her, with the bad memories and the recent storm. I was grateful to her for coming to get me here.

I took a deep breath. "All right," I said. "Let's get going, then."

She smiled and stood. I bid my farewells to Trish and Jenkins. Trish even hugged me before I left, which at first I thought seemed unprofessional. Later, I realized our professional relationship was over. I also discovered that I had grown to care about her.

Outside, the sky was starting to get dark. A group of people was there, many of whom I recognized from being in the Dry Goat before the storm. These were the Hopi—what was left of them, anyway. Many no longer bore tan skin or dark hair of their heritage, but a few did. I supposed most of them were about as pureblooded as myself.

An old man, hunched with age and carrying a twisted walking stick, approached from the crowd. I recognized him as the old man who had been smoking in the lobby of the station a couple days previously.

"This is the crow, then?" He reached out and touched my human arm with calloused fingers. His eyes sparkled in the setting sun, but it was the sparkle of intelligence and humor, not technology. "Welcome."

I tipped my hat to him.

With that, I left behind my mistakes and failures, as well as my successes. After everything that had happened, Trish had gained the respect of the people. She even had the grudging respect of the Cinco Armas and their strange leader, Court. The Brown children were arguably better off than they had been in years, and the town of Dead Oak would do about as good as could be expected. Its people would fight on.

The boy, Francis, who could turn off his pain and sadness, would grow to the notorious Francis William Brown. He would turn the world on itself. The man would end peace and tear apart any balance still left, throwing it into chaos. That is a story for another day.

This was the story of the first time I met Francis William Brown. This was the story of when I took a strange little boy and turned him into a monster.

There wasn't much justice in the world, I'd learned, but there was some. If you looked deep enough into people, you'd almost always find it. Some people, like Trish, you didn't even need to look very hard. I figured that so long as decent people still walked the desert, we would be fine. The world would move forward. Right and wrong would sort themselves out. There was justice and it didn't all come from me.

That's why I left. I would be back one day to help the world sort itself out, but at that moment I needed to figure myself out first. My mother had been part Hopi. My father had taught me the traditions of an old cowboy. It was time for me to let go of some of that, to look further back to a time when man truly lived in peace with his world. I would follow the Hopi, learn their ways. Become them.

I was no longer a peacemaker.

I was a man of peace.

Author's Note

Thank you for reading Justice in an Age of Metal and Men. A special thanks goes out to my wife Carol and my boys Isaac and Gabe. Without their support I would never have gotten this book written, edited, and published. Thanks, also, to the many others who helped and supported me along the way. Thanks go out to Scott Alexander Jones for editing and Deranged Doctor Designs for cover art.

-Anthony W. Eichenlaub

About the Author

Anthony W. Eichenlaub

Anthony is an author and software engineer from Rochester, Minnesota. His free time includes a dizzying array of hobbies such as woodworking, board games, cooking, parenting, and landscaping. He holds a degree in Computer Science as well as a Masters of Agriculture in Horticulture.

anthonyeichenlaub.com
amazon.com/author/anthonyeichenlaub
www.goodreads.com/anthony_eichenlaub
twitter.com/AWEichenlaub
https://www.facebook.com/AnthonyWEichenlaub/